THIS SIDE OF THE SUN

A New Adult Romance by

Blythe Santiago

*To Nanette
love always
Blythe Santiago*

Copyright 2014 Blythe Santiago / Larson Falls Publishing

Cover image © Artem Furman - Fotolia.com. Used under license.

This story is a work of fiction and a product of the author's imagination. Any resemblance to real people or places or events is coincidental.

Other Books by This Author

~New Adult Romance written as <u>Blythe Santiago</u>:

Coming in 2014:

(The Sun Trilogy)
Under a Brighter Sun (#2)
The Heat of a Thousand Suns (#3)

~Horror/erotic romance written as <u>M. Lauryl Lewis</u>:

Available Now:

(The Grace Series)
Grace Lost (#1)
Tainted Grace (#2)
Dark Grace (#3)
Fallen Grace (#4)
Praying for Grace (#5, coming soon)

DEDICATIONS

For my husband and our three sons, always. For Donna, and your unending polishing! For Angela- thanks for encouraging me and for believing in me!

A special "thank you" to the staff of the *Westin Ka'anapali Villas* in Maui, Hawaii. Our family stays with you often, and your beautiful grounds and kind staff inspired a portion of this story to take place in Paradise. You create a home away from home that I hope even more vacationers will come to enjoy in time. Mahalo!

CHAPTER 1 ~ SOLAR FLARE

There was no time for my usual cup of morning coffee. My brother was getting married and there was far too much to do before his noon wedding. It was a pretty Saturday in late May, but cold. Joe and Justine were going to say their vows outside on the shore, so I was glad it wasn't raining. I had volunteered to stop by Main Street Floral to pick up the flowers. Joe's best friend Everett would be his best man, and I was to be Justine's Maid of Honor. It would be a small gathering, so transporting the flowers wouldn't be difficult.

I was getting used to the jabs from friends that Joe was getting married before me. He's only younger than me by minutes, but that fact was being shoved in my face lately. I've never been big into dating. Joe's the outgoing one. I'm happy to sit in a corner with a cup of tea and read a good book. It's just the two of us now, for the most part. Our mother died delivering us twenty-one years ago. She had left our father behind to raise us on his own. He had done a fair job until we were in our teens. That's when he met our stepmother, Helen, who had made it clear after they married that she had never wanted children. She had convinced my father to live on the East Coast. Daddy divided his time between our home in Fidalgo Bay, WA, and their apartment in New York City for a while. Eventually, we seldom saw him as his visits became scarce. Now, Helen had conveniently planned a trip to Kenya and he decided to go with her rather than to his own son's wedding. Joe pretended not to care, but I knew it was really tearing him apart inside.

***

The walk from our family home to Main Street was only about two miles. I ordinarily would have ridden my Schwinn bicycle, but Joe had loaned me his car for the special occasion. I preferred getting around town on foot or by bike. I loved the fresh air, especially in Fidalgo Bay. The salt water breeze that was near constant always left me feeling refreshed.

It was early, just nine o'clock, but people were already bustling on the streets. Tourists and locals alike were milling about, enjoying the boardwalk and watching sea birds soaring nearby. Storefronts were just opening for the day and a group of musicians was setting up for a small concert for the Saturday Market. By ten o'clock there would be stands full of fresh crab, salmon, clams, oysters, and local produce lining the street. Different local bands would play throughout the day. It was like this the first and third Saturday of each month spring through summer, but would tone down to just the local seafood stands and crafts for the winter.

I parked Joe's car on the street right outside of the flower shop, unbuckled my seat belt, and slipped out of the driver's seat while no traffic was coming. A construction worker whistled at me as I stepped onto the old fashioned wooden boardwalk on my side of the street. I could feel his eyes boring holes into my butt as I walked. I recognized him as one of Joe's friends from high school. I couldn't recall his name, though. As I turned to smile and wave to him, all I saw was a bright flash of white. I wasn't aware of the searing pain in my eyes until later. An intense wave of heat hit me, throwing me backward into the building just behind me. As I fell to the ground, my head struck something hard. There was an intense ringing in my ears and my head was throbbing. I tried to breathe in, but my lungs felt as if they were on fire. I sat there, stunned, for what seemed an eternity. Just over the ringing in my ears, I could make out the sound of sirens. I opened my eyes, but was unable to see anything clearly. Smoke and debris surrounded me like a veil of imminent death.

Without warning, there was a loud noise that shook the street. Strong arms encircled me and a deep voice tried to calm me.

"Hang on, I've got you! I've got you!"

I felt myself being lifted off the ground and did the only thing that I could. I grabbed on to my savior and held on as tightly as possible as he ran with me in his arms. I choked on the toxic air around us, trying with desperation to breathe. The sirens grew louder and were accompanied by the screams and sobbing of other people. A baby was crying shrilly somewhere nearby.

"My baby! Oh God, save my baby!" screamed a woman.

"Hold on, I need to set you down. Don't move!" yelled the man who was carrying me.

"No, please don't leave me!" I yelled back, pleading.

"Stay here!" he shouted, also choking on smoke now.

He set me down as gently as he could under the circumstances. I felt cold concrete beneath me and could see a bit more clearly now. The air was clearer here, but bits of burnt matter and white ash fell to either side of me. People were running down the street, away from the destruction. The exception was the man who had just left me. He was running back into the storm of devastation. I could feel my heart beating wildly against my chest. My hands were trembling violently. I wasn't sure what had happened.

I dared to look around and was horrified to see bodies lying in the street. Some were struggling to get away from the threat of the fire and others were unmoving and surely dead. Debris littered the street and bits of burning paper swam in the air around me. The smell of burnt things stung my nose. The heat from the fire to my right was growing uncomfortable. Not knowing what else to do, I began crawling away. My left arm hurt and I saw that my sleeve was covered in blood. Before I knew what was happening, someone grabbed onto my right hand and pulled me up until I was standing.

"I thought I told you to stay put!"

I looked to the man who had just scolded me. He was a bit taller than me and had dark wavy hair. His bright blue eyes were reddened from the smoke. His face was rugged, sporting a five-o-clock shadow, and was smeared with soot. He was holding a tiny infant in the crook of his other arm, still loosely swaddled in a light pink receiving blanket. It hurt my throat to speak, so I just looked forward in reply.

"Keep running!" he yelled. "As fast as you can! Don't look back!"

He was pulling me forward, and I held tightly onto his large hand. His voice was deep and commanding, but he could have been a rodeo clown trying to sell used tires and I would have done as told. The tiny baby in his arm was wailing.

"C'mon, faster!" he barked with a sense of urgency.

The street before us had grown crowded. People of all shapes and sizes, all colors, all ages were running away from the destruction. At first it appeared that a medic was running toward us, but just as quickly his face contorted and he turned to run. The man pulling me forward gripped my hand even harder, almost painfully so. Behind us, a wave of heat and pressure pushed us forward. I stumbled to my knees, but the man never let go of my hand. Screams of agony and cries of sorrow surrounded us, along with the rumble of buildings on fire.

"What's happened?" I yelled from where I had fallen.

The man beside me crouched down and was covering the baby and myself the best he could with his own body.

"Some kind of explosion! We have to get farther away! We have to run again! Are you ready?"

I looked into his striking blue eyes and nodded. We stood together and ran again, still holding hands. The heat from the blaze behind us was near searing. It was hard to breathe and my eyes felt like they were on fire.

CHAPTER 2 ~ JUST BREATHE

Finally, after following others in hopes of finding safety, we arrived at a safe zone that had been set up for triaging victims. We were several blocks east of the burning block of buildings by now. Medics, fire fighters, and police had quickly organized tents and mobile treatment units. A sheriff was suddenly at our side, and took the baby from my savior. She was yelling for us to follow her.

The man beside me, his other arm now freed, lifted me from the ground and walked quickly to the closest tent. Setting me on a portable table, he looked into my eyes. At that moment, his eyes were the only thing I could see. Not the death and destruction and terrors that surrounded us. Just the kindness in his eyes.

"I think I'm going to pass out," I mumbled, feeling light headed.

"Shhh, just breathe," he soothed. "Just breathe." I felt his hand gently smoothing the hair on the back of my head.

I did as instructed, taking a breath in. As the cool sea air filled my lungs, I began coughing again. Almost immediately a medic was at my side and placed an oxygen mask over my face.

The medic looked at the man who was still at my side. I realized I was still clutching onto his hand. "Wrap the elastic strap around her head?" suggested the medic. "Stay here with her?"

The man nodded in reply as the medic rushed off to help an old woman who looked as if she may die at any moment.

"You saved me," I said through the plastic mask.

"I suppose I did." He smiled softly at me. "What's your name?"

I coughed again, which prompted him to rub me gently on the back.

"Don't talk if it's too hard. Just breathe the oxygen. I'm Saul. Saul Meyers."

I tried to slow my breathing and focused on watching others pass by. So many of them looked in such terrible shape. Blood, burns, tears. Faces full of grief and pain.

"Hattie," I said, my voice muffled by the mask.

"Nice to meet you, Patty," said Saul.

I took the mask off of my face. "No," I whispered hoarsely. "Hattie."

Saul smiled down at me. "Well that's even prettier. Pleasure to meet you, Hattie. Pretty crappy circumstances, though."

I continued to breathe the oxygen and nodded my agreement. Saul lifted my left arm and began looking for the cause of the bleeding.

"Ah, here it is," he said calmly. "Nothing a Band-Aid won't cure."

His smile was charming, and more importantly I found it to be calming. I watched his face as he inspected my wound. He was ruggedly handsome. I figured he was in his mid-twenties but I didn't dare ask him.

Things around us were slowly starting to calm down. Fewer people were running, but fire fighters were struggling to contain the inferno down the street. Wounds and burns were being tended to in order of severity. I wondered briefly what had become of the baby that Saul had saved. Breathing was getting easier. I took my mask off and looked around. There were people far worse off than me.

"I think I should leave," I said somberly.

"You really need to get looked at."

"It's easier to breathe now, though. And my arm isn't that bad. I can clean it at home. Look at these people. They need help way more than I do."

Saul did as I suggested and looked around us.

"I suppose you're right. But it'd be irresponsible of me to just let you walk off. Let me at least see you home?"

"I wouldn't usually say yes to a stranger, but under the circumstances I'd really appreciate it. My brother's car was back there where you found me."

I'm parked about four blocks up. Do you think you can walk that far?"

I nodded. "I think so."

"And you don't feel like you're hurt anywhere else?"

I shook my head no.

"Ok, Miss Hattie. We should at least leave our names with someone."

I coughed one more time and nodded.

"I'll find someone. You wait here. Oh, what's your last name?"

"Leonardo."

"Alright, Hattie Leonardo, stay put and I'll be right back."

He winked at me, causing me to flush.

***

Several minutes later, Saul returned to where I was perched and offered me his hand. I took it, this time aware that it was an offer of kindness and not one of necessity. I took it willingly.

"Sorry that took so long. I left our names with one of the local police. Let's get out of here," he said.

I just nodded. My throat was still sore. We began walking in the general direction of where he had left his truck. Self-conscious, I had let my hand slip out of his as we walked. I didn't want to hurt his feelings, so pretended I had an itch on my other arm. As much as I appreciated his saving my life, he was a handsome man and I was chronically shy.

"You doing ok?" he asked me.

"Yes, just a bit sore."

Saul stopped walking and put his hands on his hips. "Are you hurting somewhere?" He seemed genuinely concerned.

"No, just achy."

"You sure you can walk? We'll be there soon, but I can bring the truck back for you."

The thought of this stranger leaving my side sent me into near-panic.

"No, no," I fumbled for words. "I'll be fine. Really."

"You look a little pale."

I chucked nervously. "I'm always pale."

From the few pictures I had of my mother, I assumed I got her pale skin and splattering of faint freckles that darkened every summer. I was cursed with my father's wavy light brown hair. It's between straight and curly and rather 'blah.'

"Well, it suits your big green eyes," he said with a soft smile.

Feeling my face flush, I managed to mumble a quick "thanks."

"Okay, let's get you home."

We began walking again. Smoke was lingering in the air, drifting our direction in the breeze. Sirens were piercing the air as more trucks came to battle the blaze and ambulances transported people from the triage site to local hospitals. Helicopters were hovering overhead, likely filming for local news stations. One was larger than the rest. I paused to watch as it landed behind a building that was obstructing our view.

"It's a medic helicopter," explained Saul. He had to yell next to me over the noise of the huge copter. "Let's hurry before the roads get jammed up."

He grabbed my hand again and urged me forward. We heard an explosion in the distance behind us.

"Just one more block," he promised. "Almost there." He was obviously in a hurry and trying to keep his cool for my sake.

Saul had me near-running now. We reached the truck in short order and he used his key fob to unlock it. As he opened the driver's door, another explosion rocked the ground upon which we stood.

"Hattie, get in and scoot over!" he yelled urgently.

Without hesitating, I stepped up onto the runner board and climbed into the front seat, clambering over the center console to make room for the man who was right behind me. I could feel adrenaline coursing through my veins. Saul jumped in before I was fully in the passenger seat, slamming his door shut. He quickly inserted the key into the ignition and the engine purred to life. I didn't dare speak until we were moving forward.

"Saul? What's going on?"

"I'm not really sure, but I think the fire just got a heck of a lot worse. We probably got out of there just in time."

His face was full of intense tension. I looked behind us. There was a huge plume of dark black smoke rising high into the sky. The helicopter that had landed was back in the air and fighting for stability as it moved away from the area.

"Hang on, Hattie."

The truck began speeding away. I looked forward and wiped at my eyes, which had become filled with tears. People seeing me cry was never something I had appreciated.

"Take a deep breath. We're ok."

"Do you think all those people just died?" I asked in a shaky voice.

He stole a quick glance at me and then looked forward again.

"Possibly."

I noticed that Saul was gripping the steering wheel tightly with both hands, and his knuckles were white. Now several blocks farther away, he slowed a bit and pulled off of the road and into the parking lot of a local café.

"Think we're far enough to be safe?" I asked.

"Yeah. I just need to clear my head for a minute. Well, and figure out where I'm taking you."

"I can't stop thinking of all the people back there." I wiped at my face again.

Saul opened his door and stepped out. He closed it gently and walked to the back of the truck. I stayed in the cab and tried to slow my breathing and keep more tears from falling. Stealing a glance in the side mirror, I saw that Saul was near the tailgate, facing away, his hands on his knees. I knew then that he, too, was badly shaken. I opened my own door and slid out and down to the ground. I slowly walked toward my new companion. Sensing me, he stood up and attempted to compose himself. Turning halfway to face me, he kicked at a large metal dumpster that was beside him.

"Fuck," he yelled. "FUCK!"

I flinched, not expecting the outburst.

"I'm sorry," I muttered.

He turned the rest of the way to face me and laughed, rather inappropriately.

"No way. You have nothing to be sorry about." He took a deep breath and looked up to the sky for a moment. "Yes, I think most of those people died."

Finally, he looked back to me.

"We almost died," I said quietly.

"Yeah, we almost died." He took a deep breath. "Sorry for my cursing."

I began shaking. I wasn't really sure what to do.

"Look at you. You're in shock. We need to get you warmed up. Think you can tell me how to get you home?"

I nodded while watching him walk to the passenger side of his truck. He opened the door and reached behind the seat, pulling out a zip-up hoodie.

"Here, wrap this around yourself. I promise to not kick and scream again."

"Ok." I let him drape the large sweatshirt over my shoulders, and let him help me up into the truck since this side didn't have a runner board. I welcomed the warmth of his hands on my hips as he helped boost me into the cab.

A moment later, he appeared in the driver's seat.

"Go back the way you were headed. Then turn right on Maple."

"You got it."

We drove on in relative silence. The sirens and helicopters still lingered, but not as loudly as before.

"Head this way till you get to 13th, then go left."

"So what were you doing in town?" he asked.

"Picking up flowers for my brother's wedding."

"Is it today?"

"Yeah."

"Guess this'll put a crimp in their plans?"

"I suppose you're right," I answered with a sigh. "How about you?"

"I didn't have plans today."

I stifled a chuckle. "No, I meant what were you doing in town?"

"Oh, just grabbing a coffee."

"So do you live here?"

"Just moved here a couple weeks ago. Got sick of the big city so decided to move into a little beach bungalow. It's more of a shack, really. Belonged to my grandfather."

"Like it so far?"

"Well enough. I have some good memories of the place."

"Oh, we just passed 12th. It's the next left," I said as we got close to the turn off to my house.

As Saul turned left onto 13th, I wondered if anyone would be home. They might all be at the wedding already, wondering where the flowers were.

"Do you know what time it is? I think I lost my cell phone back there."

He checked his watch, something I had never taken a liking to wearing myself.

"Ten till noon."

"Already? Guess I'm gonna be late for the wedding."

"When is it?"

"Noon."

"I wouldn't worry about being on time, Hattie. They'll all just be glad you're alive."

"I suppose so." I paused. "That's my house on the left. The light blue Cape Cod."

Saul pulled his truck onto the street two houses down. My driveway was packed with cars, as was the street. They should all be miles away at the shore, getting ready for Joe and Justine to say their vows.

"Looks like there's a crowd waiting for you," said Saul.

"I don't want to go in," I admitted. I hated being the center of attention and didn't want to talk about the events of the day.

"Do you want me to come with you?" he offered.

I looked at him in surprise. "You've already done too much for me."

"You sure you'll be ok?"

"Yeah. How about you?"

He sighed deeply. "I'll be fine, but I'm pretty pissed off, to be honest."

"Yeah."

"I wish I could have saved more people."

"Thanks for saving me," I whispered. "Sorry, that sounded dumb."

"No, not at all. You're welcome. And I'm glad I did save you, and those beautiful green eyes."

He turned in his seat to face me, lifted a hand, and cupped my cheek in his palm. I closed my eyes for a moment and leaned into his touch, needing to just feel human contact; to make sure I was alive. The enormity of the morning was starting to settle in.

When I heard him speak, I opened my eyes.

"Here's your crowd."

I turned to look toward my house and saw Joe rushing toward the truck. My heart began pounding, not wanting to face the attention I was about to receive. I looked back at Saul, my eyes wide with fear.

"You'll be fine," he soothed. "Here, take this. Call me if you need to talk, okay? Anytime, day or night."

He handed me a business card. I took it and smiled. "Thanks. I will."

"Okay, hop out and let them know you're alright."

"Thanks, Saul" I said humbly. "For everything."

"Anytime," he said with a wink.

I opened the passenger door and slid out. Joe was there waiting, and immediately embraced me.

"Oh God, Hattie, you're ok!" he sobbed.

Choking up myself, I was unable to answer. I heard Saul's truck pull away from the curb and felt my heart sink a bit.

CHAPTER 3 ~ HOMECOMING

"Hattie, we've been trying to call," cried Joe. "I was so afraid you had…" he choked on the words, unable to say his entire thought out loud.

"Joe, get her inside. There's time to talk later." It was Miranda, Everett's mom. She had been the closest thing I'd had to a mother growing up. Everett had been Joe's best friend since kindergarten. He'd made it clear before that he hoped we'd get married and live happily ever after. He's always been like a brother to me, though. I had never let our relationship go beyond that.

"Thank God you're alive," moaned Joe.

I still hadn't said a word. I wasn't sure I could, to be honest. As Joe and Justine each held onto my arms and guided me to the front door, I clutched Saul's business card tightly in my fist. As we entered the living room, several people stood to greet us. Some of them I knew, some of them I didn't. There was a chorus of praises that I was home and alive. It was overwhelming. I wanted more than anything to be alone.

"Someone make some hot tea," instructed Miranda. "And get a blanket. The poor thing must be in shock."

Someone led me to the sofa, where I sat gratefully. A blanket was wrapped around my shoulders, making me realize I was still wearing Saul's hoodie. Someone tried to take the paper from my hand.

"No!" I yelled, startling everyone in the room. "No! Don't take it!"

"Hattie, shhh, it's ok," said Joe.

"No, it's not," I said. "None of it is."

I stood up, letting the blanket fall behind me onto the couch. I turned quickly and walked out of the room, my arms crossed, and climbed the stairs that led to the peace of my own bedroom. I didn't look back at the unwanted crowd.

"Hattie!" I heard Joe call out as I reached the landing at the top of the steps.

I paused for just a moment but didn't look back. I walked forward and turned left into the bathroom. I shut the door quietly and locked the old fashioned lever knob. I turned so that my back faced the door and slid down until I was sitting on the cold granite floor. I drew my legs up to my chest and wrapped my arms around them. I wanted to climb into a cold, dark hole. I wanted to be alone, for the house full of people to just go away. I didn't want to cry or yell or scream or sleep. I just wanted to be alone.

I closed my eyes, laid my head on my knees, and took a deep, shuddering breath. The slight knock on the door behind me was startling, sending my heart racing.

"Hattie, Honey, it's Miranda. Can I come in?" Her voice was soft and caring. "Please?"

I sighed quietly and then stood. My muscles were even stiffer than before. I turned back to the bathroom door and quietly unlocked it. I turned the knob and pulled it open as I backed up.

"Oh, Hattie, my dear sweet Hattie," cooed Miranda. "Oh, sweetie, look at you."

She wrapped her slender arms around me tightly. It wasn't the first motherly gesture she had made in my lifetime and I welcomed her closeness.

"What happened, Miranda?" I asked, sounding lost.

"They haven't announced the cause yet. It's a major blaze, though. There's been at least three explosions. Oh, Hattie, we'd all thought we'd lost you."

Miranda began crying on my shoulder.

"Joe's car is gone," I muttered.

"Oh Lord, no one cares about the car. We're just all so thankful you're alive." She stepped back from me and placed her hands on my shoulders. "You're filthy. And your arm…"

"It's ok. It's just a scratch."

"Let me draw you a bath, Sugar. Let's get you cleaned up and into bed."

"The wedding…" I started to say, but was interrupted.

"Hattie, the wedding will happen another day." Joe had walked up behind Miranda. "Don't even think about that now," he insisted. "Everyone's gone home except Everett and Justine. Let's just get you taken care of."

I nodded. "I'm sorry about your car, Joey."

"Stop about the car," ordered Miranda, who had walked to the large claw foot tub and began to fill it with hot water and a splash of lavender oil.

"Yup. Stop about the car. None of that's important," echoed Joe.

"Ok, Sug, leave your filthy clothes on the floor and I'll come get them in a few minutes. I'll bring a clean towel in with me."

"Thanks, Miranda."

She gently moved Joe out of the doorway and shut the door behind her. I took a breath and tried to shut off my mind. I looked down at my fist and realized I was still clutching at Saul's business card. I placed it on the back of the white pedestal sink and then dared a glance in the mirror. I was a horrific sight. The skin of my face was beet red, much like a sunburn, and smeared with soot and tears. My hair was stringy and half out of its ponytail. I nearly didn't recognize myself. I brought my hands up to my face and placed the cuffs of the dingy hoodie under my nose, very much like I would do with my childhood blanket when I was young. I was surprised that it smelled of fabric softener. It looked filthy but I could tell Saul had just washed it. When the scent of lavender started to mingle with that of Downy, I looked over to the bath and was surprised it was already half full of steaming water. I slipped out of the hoodie first and hung it on the hook that was mounted on the back of the door. I slid out of my loose crinkled skirt and pulled my t-shirt over my head. My muscles were still sore and the thought of the warm water was appealing. Finally, I slid out of my under things and left everything, including my shoes, on the floor as Miranda had instructed. I slid into the bath water with care. It was hot enough to sting, but I needed to feel the pain. My left arm took the worst of the assault. The shallow wound on my arm felt like it was on fire when submerged beneath the water. I winced and closed my eyes before slipping down in the tub until the water was covering my shoulders. Eventually the aches and pains eased. At least the physical ones. I heard the door open once, but kept my eyes closed. I knew it would be Miranda collecting my soiled clothes.

As much as I tried to enjoy the hot soak, images and sounds of the morning kept filling my mind. The crying baby. The screaming mother. The flames.

People running for their lives. The masks of fear everyone wore. I wish I could make the memories stop. I slid under the water, holding my breath, and stayed in the quiet calm for as long as I could. Coming up for air, I wiped the water from my eyes and looked around the room. I was home. I was alive. I was safe now. I just wished I felt it: safe. Miranda had left a clean towel on the shelf for me. I quickly washed my hair and face and dunk one more time to rinse off. I used a washcloth to gently scrub at my arm. The scratch still looked angry, but at least the blood and dirt were now gone. I unplugged the drain and stepped out of the tub. Melting into my own bed was all I really wanted to do now. I wrapped in the fluffy burgundy towel, retrieved Saul's business card from the sink, and left the steamy bathroom behind.

When I reached my bedroom, I was relieved to see that no one was waiting for me. Someone had set out a pair of flannel pajamas. I searched through my drawers for a pair of panties and got dressed. I turned the covers back and sat on the edge of the bed staring at the card in my hands. Sighing, I opened my night stand drawer and tucked the card away. There was a glass of water and a small bowl sitting on top of the bedside table, as well as a hand written note.

Hattie, we're so glad you're ok. Take this Tylenol before you go to sleep.
I'll check on you later.   *–Justine*

I gratefully swallowed the pills, and then slid under the covers. I brought them up to my chin and curled into a ball.

***

When I woke, it was full dark outside. The only light was coming from the digital alarm clock beside the bed. I was confused at first. My eyes were dry, as was my mouth. I sat up in bed, feeling the ache of every muscle in my body. That pain is what reminded me of what had happened. My heart started pounding and it was hard to catch my breath. I still didn't know what exactly had happened downtown. The clock beside me said it was 4:04. I slid out of bed and walked to the closet, searching for my bathrobe. I found it quickly, wrapped it around myself, and slid into my favorite pair of slippers. I quietly opened my door and walked down the stairs, not wanting to wake anyone. I snuck into the kitchen and took out a bottle of water, which I drank from greedily. I took what was left of the water and slipped into the living room, hoping to turn the news on.

Everett was sleeping on the couch, his arm hanging over the edge. He was snoring lightly. I assumed that Justine was in Joe's room with him, which left me wondering where Miranda was. Since this was the only television we had in the house, I sat on the floor in front of the only ottoman in the room and used the remote to turn on the flat screen. It was one rare luxury we had splurged on. Daddy sent home money until we turned eighteen, but his wife had cut that off as her birthday gift to us. We both worked, but neither of us made very good money, so we had a tendency to be frugal. Joe did maintenance for the local school district, which consisted of only two elementary schools, one middle, and one high. I worked as a barista, but it was only part time every Wednesday through Friday. I'd still watch the kids down the street, Aimee and Amanda, about once a month. I'm sure she'd gladly sell it if she could. And now the café where I had worked had burnt down. The house was paid for and we had a right to it from our mother's will, so Helen couldn't touch that

As the screen warmed up and began to light up the room, I hit the volume button to keep it quiet, not wanting to wake Everett. I clicked through the major stations until I found one featuring the tragedy from the day before. It mostly showed clips from earlier in the day, always from a distance. It had seemed worse in person, likely because I had been in the middle of it all, up close and personal. The news woman was talking about speculations still. It was an assumed gas line explosion. Since one of the neighboring buildings housed propane, it was also assumed that was responsible for the after-explosions. Still, no one knew for sure just yet what the actual cause was. They were anticipating a lengthy investigation and that area of the town would be out of commission until it could be rebuilt. They were predicting an economic hardship for the area. The death toll was still coming in, but currently at twenty confirmed lost. There were six people in critical condition at Harborview Hospital in Seattle, and at least another sixteen at local area hospitals with varying degrees of injuries. The gravity of the situation began to hit me like a ton of bricks, as did the reality that I very well could have been included in that death toll. Not to mention the tiny baby Saul had gone back for. I wasn't ready to shed tears. I wasn't sure what I wanted or needed to do. I took a deep breath and hung my head.

The sofa behind me squeaked. Startled, I turned to see Everett sitting up.

"Everett, I'm sorry. I didn't mean to wake you."

"You ok, Hat?"

I shrugged. "I guess. A little sore."

He stood and walked over to me.

"That's not what I mean. You've been through a lot. Are you ok, like, emotionally?"

I bit my lip and cracked my knuckles. "I think so. Glad to be alive."

Soon he sat beside me and wrapped an arm around me. "Me too, Hattie. Me too."

His embrace felt like just a bit more than that of a friend, and made me tense slightly.

"Where'd your mom go?"

"She had to go home to take care of the dog. She said she'd be back and make us all breakfast."

"That's nice of her."

"Did you want to talk about what happened?"

I shook my head as he tightened his arm.

"Ok, but let me know if you need me to lend an ear, ok?"

"Thanks, Everett."

I smiled at him. As I started to turn my head away he put his palm on my cheek. I knew by the look in his eyes that he was looking at me not as a friend or a sister, but rather as someone he might love. My core went cold as he leaned in, presumably trying to kiss me.

I backed away just a bit. "Everett…"

He sighed and looked at me, not letting go of my face.

"I'm sorry," I said. "It's just…things are really crazy right now. I can't handle more craziness on top of it all."

He took his other hand and put it on the other side of my face. "I'm sorry, Hat."

I put my own hand over one of his. "I know. I should go back to bed."

He nodded and slowly let go of my face. "I think I'll go for a run. See you in the morning?"

"Yeah, sure."

We both stood and went our separate ways. The last thing I wanted to do was hurt him.

CHAPTER 4 ~ THE SIMPLE THINGS

I went back to bed and managed to sleep for a couple more hours. I woke to the smell of cooking bacon and coffee. I knew that Miranda must have returned, so I drug myself out of bed and dressed in a pair of tight cotton exercise pants and a t-shirt before heading across the hall to use the bathroom. I was ravenous and anxious to get downstairs to eat, which made my trip to the bathroom brief. My hair in a messy ponytail, I hurried down the stairs despite sore muscles from the day before.

"Mornin' Glory!" chirped Miranda when she saw me enter the kitchen. "You're just in time for breakfast."

"Hey sis," said Joe. "Get some sleep?"

"A bit. Any news on what happened yesterday?" I asked. My need to know was growing.

"They said investigating could take weeks," said Justine after swallowing her coffee.

"Hattie, have you seen Everett?" asked Joe.

I sat down in an empty chair at the kitchen table and looked up as Miranda handed me a cup of tea. "Thanks, Miranda." I looked at Joe as I blew the steam away from the top of the mug.

"Everett?" asked Joe again.

"He went for a run early this morning," I said simply. I wondered if somehow Joe knew about my little incident with Everett during the night.

"Did I hear my name?" I heard Everett say as he shut the front door. He was still dressed in spandex shorts and a tank top from his run. He grinned at me, a little longer than made me comfortable. I buried my head in my cup of tea, sipping at it even though it was still far too hot.

"So, Justine and I have some news," said Joe.

I looked up, grateful for the distraction.

"Oh?" asked Miranda.

Joe joined Justine, standing behind her at the table. "We've decided to go ahead with the wedding. We're heading to the Justice of the Peace today."

"Aw, man, you sure you two want to do that?" asked Everett.

Miranda promptly elbowed her son in the ribs to warn him to shut up. "I think it's a fine idea. It's the simple things that matter in life, right?"

"Where will you go?" I asked. "The court house is gone."

Fidalgo Bay had one of the smallest court houses in the state, but it had been downtown in the line of the explosions. It'd be either burnt down or off limits now.

"We'll head in to Anacortes. I already checked online and they have open hours today."

"It's Sunday, though," I remarked.

Justine looked up at my brother and smiled. She always looked so in love when around him. "The courthouse itself is closed for the weekend but the JOP is private. We're hoping you'll all come as witnesses?" Her blue eyes sparkled. "If you feel up to it, Hattie?"

I nodded. In truth, I wanted to go back to bed and loaf in my pajamas all day and feel sorry for myself, but I couldn't say no. "Sure I do. I wouldn't miss my baby brother's wedding for anything!"

Justine beamed. "Good! Two o'clock it is then."

"I'll be ready," I mumbled into the mug in my hands as I took another sip.

"We should eat," said Miranda. "Bacon and eggs anyone?"

"I think I'll just have a slice of toast," I mumbled. "And maybe a piece of bacon. And maybe some eggs," I added.

"Hungry?" asked Joe snidely.

I rolled my eyes at him dramatically and then smiled.

I was finding it hard to think about anything but the events of the day before. Eventually someone set a plate in front of me with two buttered pieces of wheat toast, scrambled eggs, and two slices of crispy bacon. I ate, pretending to listen to Justine as she rattled off her plans for the day. They would be spending the next couple nights in a bed and breakfast just outside of Anacortes. Miranda offered to either stay in our home with me, or for me to come bunk with her and Everett for a while. I politely declined the offer, assuring her I'd be fine by myself. Once I was done with my plate of food, I carried it to the sink and rinsed it off, and then stacked it inside the dishwasher. It was already eight o'clock so I excused myself to go nap and then prepare for the impromptu wedding.

***

It had taken me awhile to wash and dry my hair and set it in hot curlers. Make-up was something I seldom wore, so I took my time with it to make sure it looked alright. I finished with light pink lipstick. Once the rollers had cooled, I unrolled them and shook my head to loosen the resulting curls. I braided two small sections on either side of my head and tied them together in the back with a small clear rubber band. It would have to do. Wrapped in a bath towel, I snuck back into my bedroom. I picked out a strapless white bra, matching panties, and an ivory sundress covered in large yellow sunflowers. I added simple pearl earrings that had belonged to my mother and white strappy sandals.

"Hattie, you ready?" called someone from below.

"Yeah, just a sec!"

I walked back to the bathroom and found a large flesh-colored Band-Aid and covered the angry scratch on my arm. I took one last look in the mirror. I wasn't thrilled with my reflection. I looked okay, I supposed, but after the explosion my face still looked slightly burnt.

"Hattie!" yelled Everett. "Speed it up, girl!"

I rolled my eyes and moved to the hallway. At the last minute I rushed back into my bedroom and fetched the stained hoodie Saul had left with me. I bundled it beneath my elbow and hustled down the stairs. Everett was waiting for me by the front door. He cat-whistled as I came into view.

I rolled my eyes at him.

"Everyone left already. I offered to stay and wait for you."

"Thanks," I said suspiciously.

He opened the door for me, and I walked out into the overcast day. As the door slammed behind us, I jumped.

"Hey, it was just the door," said Everett in a soothing voice.

I looked at him for a moment before nodding.

He put a hand on my shoulder. "You okay?"

"Yeah. Just a little freaked out after yesterday."

He stepped closer and embraced me. I didn't push him away, but didn't return the affection.

"It'll take time, Hat."

He nuzzled his nose against my cheek, kissing just beside my mouth. His warm lips barely touched my skin and his breathing sounded different. I tensed, but he kept me in his arms for a lingering moment. He smelled of linen and after shave.

I finally found my voice. "We should go."

He unwrapped his arms from me and backed away like nothing had happened. He walked briskly to his station wagon. I had teased him about that old wood-paneled car for a couple years now. As he stood next to the passenger door holding it open for me, I took notice of how handsome he looked. Dark gray suit, white linen collared shirt, and a sage green silk tie. It was quite a contrast to his usual frayed blue jeans and off the wall t-shirts. He even had his reddish-blonde hair combed into a part and swept to one side.

I walked to the open door and slid in, allowing Everett to shut the door behind me. I buckled my seat belt and folded my hands on my lap. Soon Everett was sitting beside me and the engine rumbled to life, after only a couple of sputters. I kept my gaze forward, feeling slightly uncomfortable, but felt his eyes on me. Eventually the awkward moment ended when he pulled the car onto the street and headed toward the town of Anacortes.

I didn't feel much like talking, so listened half-heartedly as Everett told me about his latest work gripes. He had been promoted and had to let an employee go for stealing. It sounded like the kid had been a trouble maker from the get-go. Now he'd be looking for a new welder.

Eventually we arrived outside the courthouse. The street reminded me too much of the street I had been on just yesterday. It sent shivers up my arms. Joe was on the sidewalk waiting for us and opened my door. He was dressed as nicely as Everett. I stepped out of the car and hustled inside since the wind was kicking up and splatters of rain drops were just starting to fall. Justine was waiting inside, dressed in a simple ankle-length white satin sleeveless dress. She looked stunningly beautiful. Miranda was at her side, dressed in a simple light blue suit trimmed in white. She was the kind of woman who was aging nicely and always looked nice. She could have been wearing a burlap sack and still been stunning.

We waited for only twenty minutes before being called in to a large office with a high ceiling and an ornately carved cherry wood desk. The Justice of the Peace sat behind the desk, smiling. He was an older man with gray hair and a kind smile. The ceremony took all of ten minutes. Everett and I signed the marriage certificate as witnesses.

Mr. and Mrs. Joe Leonardo looked ecstatic. Hugs were given freely and just when we were about to send them off to celebrate their wedding night, Justine surprised us.

"Joe and I are heading out to a local pub before hitting up the B & B. Come with us?"

I looked at Joe questioningly. "Justine, don't you two want to be alone?" I asked

Joe laughed. "Come out with us. Just for a couple hours. Celebrate."

I really didn't want to go anywhere but home and back to bed. I sighed. "Ok. But just for a little while."

Miranda excused herself to head back home. She had driven herself, so that left me at the mercy of Everett and his beast of a station wagon. I thought briefly about running after her as she drove away, begging for her to take me with her.

"Ok, I'll change in the car," chirped Justine. Meet you guys at Blarney's? It's just around the corner and two blocks up."

Everett and Joe fist-bumped before we headed out. I sat in the car while Everett took his suit jacket and tie off and unbuttoned his linen shirt for a more relax feel. I wondered how Justine would change out of her dress and into something else inside her small coupe. Everett pulled back onto the street and headed in the direction of the pub.

CHAPTER 5 ~ LET ME DROWN

Blarney's Pub was one of the oddest establishments in which I had ever been. The entry and front area looked like a combination of a traditional bar and grill with dart boards and a few pull tab machines. There were flying pig motifs everywhere. There was a narrow stairway off to the left that led down to a lower level. A sign at the top made it clear that beyond was meant for those twenty-one and over. Everett told me that Justine and Joe would be waiting down there. I descended the steps first. Swirls of light from a disco ball blinded me at first. The atmosphere was completely different from the upstairs. Walls were painted a flat black, or maybe it was a dark blue. Lighting was dim and indirect. Booths lined three of the walls; their seats were plush deep purple velvet. There were also old fashioned overstuffed chairs and couches in the same fabric, but in blue and deep green, scattered around the periphery between booths. The far wall held a bar that ran nearly the length of the room and was under recessed blue lighting. I had never been in a venue like this and instantly felt out of place. Everett took hold of my elbow and led me to a booth off to one side.

"I'm sure they'll be here soon," he whispered as he slid in beside me. There were a handful of other patrons around us. It was still early in the day; mid-afternoon. I supposed it'd be crowded before much longer. Music was playing loudly: Indie Rock I hadn't heard before. I had never been a fan of loud music but figured I'd tolerate it for the sake of my brother and his new wife.

A slim waitress wearing tight black shorts and a lacy red halter-top approached us with a seductive smile, aimed right at Everett. I avoided laughing, not wanting to be rude.

"Welcome to Barney's Below. My name's Ginger. Can I get you two anything to drink?"

Everett slipped an arm around my shoulders and beamed at the waitress named 'Ginger.'

"A bottle of your best champagne and four glasses, please."

"Excellent. Celebrating?" she asked.

"We sure are. My friend just got hitched! They'll be joining us anytime."

I removed Everett's hand from my shoulder.

"May I also have a glass of water, please?" I asked Miss Halter-Top. "No ice?"

"You bet, Honey. Oh, I'll need to see your ID's."

We both produced our driver's licenses. Ginger looked at mine briefly and had a slight look of disappointment in realizing I was indeed twenty-one. She spent more time studying Everett's, probably trying to memorize his address. He seemed oblivious to her obvious flirting.

Ginger returned to the table with a bottle of champagne in a silver bucket of ice and four red-toned crystal flutes.

"Okay, handsome, would you like me to open and pour or do y'all want the pleasure?" Ginger spoke sweetly to Everett right as Joe and Justine walked up to our table.

"We're good, thanks," interrupted Joe.

Ginger took her leave as Justine slid into the booth ahead of Joe, leaving behind a towel for opening the champagne. Everett put the crisp white linen towel across his arm as he reached for the bottle of bubbly. He fiddled with the metal foil that covered the bottle, eventually untwisting the wire that held the cap in place. Once he had it freed, the resulting pop of the cork flying across the room startled me. Images of the fire and explosions returned to my mind as Everett began filling the glasses.

"Hattie? You okay?" asked Joe as he reached across the table and took my hand.

I looked up and nodded.

"A toast," said Everett. "To Joseph and Justine Leonardo. May all your days be happy and bright."

Glasses clinked and I sipped eagerly at my drink, which was highly unlike me. I felt a need to numb something inside of myself, though. Finishing the glass without stopping, I got a few sideways glances from my companions.

"Slow down, Hat," whispered Everett. "We have all night."

I looked at him with exaggerated irritation and held my empty glass up for more. "I think after yesterday I deserve a few hours off."

He poured a second glass for me, smirking as he did so.

"You know," said Justine. "You two make a cute couple."

I had started to drink round two and choked into my glass. "Not funny, Justine. We're just friends." My face was feeling hot, partly from the first glass of alcohol and partly from embarrassment.

"Don't embarrass her, Jus," said Everett.

I tipped my glass of champagne back and swallowed the rest. It was immediately refilled, by Justine.

"Slow down," mumbled my brother. "You have all night, Sis."

I rolled my eyes at him, but took heed of his warning and sipped at my drink. Everett and Joe began talking about the explosions the day before. Justine nudged me under the table with her foot and promptly made a motion with her head toward Everett. I just shook my head back and forth in a clear gesture of 'no.' She was the only one still working on her first glass of champagne.

Ginger the Halter-Whore returned to the table, with a slightly younger version of herself tagging along.

"We all doing ok?" she asked with a fake smile.

I could tell she had refreshed her make-up as well. She stood a little too close to Everett. I had always hated when others referenced 'we' instead of 'you,' somehow trying to include themselves into the equation when they weren't.

"Just fine," answered Joe a bit too enthusiastically. "We could use four shots of Jägermeister, though."

"Very nice choice," said the new girl.

"This is Britnee," explained Ginger. "I'm off in ten, so she'll be taking over for me."

Britnee, like Ginger, was dressed in tight black shorts and a halter top. Britnee's was lavender, though, and had a difficult time containing her ample bosoms. It was hard not to stare.

"Thanks for all your help, Ginger," said Everett. I had to keep myself from laughing. As Britnee walked back to the bar to gather the next round of drinks, I noticed that Ginger slipped Everett a small piece of paper before winking at him and walking away with an extra little swing to her hips.

"Gee, that was subtle," groaned Justine.

I was the first to toss back my shot of dark German liquor. It tasted far too much like cough medicine. I was enjoying feeling numb, though, and stole Everett's shot before he got around to drinking it.

"Let's get more," I said, my speech a bit slurred.

"I think you've had enough, Sis. Justine and I are heading off for our wedding night. Everett, can you make sure she gets home ok?" He gestured toward me.

"Of course, Bro."

"C'mon, Wife," said Joe with a shit-eating grin.

He stood, offering a hand to his new bride. They snuck off, up the stairs, and were off for their big night; leaving me alone with Everett.

"Just you and me, huh?" he said.

"We should get going too," I said.

"We're here, might as well have some fun," he said as he slid closer and put his arm around me again.

"Everett, no. I told you last night…"

"C'mon, Hattie. We've known each other since what…forever?"

He raised an arm, calling Britnee over.

She responded promptly. "You two need anything? Your friends left an open tab and said it's all on them."

"Ah, that was sweet of them. See, Hat, we need to stay and enjoy their gift."

"How about some food?" suggested Britnee.

"Mmm, yeah, good idea. Hattie, what would you like?"

"I'm not hungry."

People were starting to crowd into the room for the evening and the volume of the music had increased.

"How about I put together a sample platter of appetizers?" suggested the waitress, who I already liked a lot more than I had Ginger.

"That'd be great," said Everett. "Thank you. Oh and one more bottle of champagne."

Britnee nodded and then took her leave back to the bar to submit the order.

"Everett...I've had enough to drink. And I'm not hungry."

He sighed heavily, obviously irritated with me. "Ok, I get it. You're not attracted to me. Let's just hang out as friends?"

"Come on, Ev. That's not fair. You're hot and you know it. But, you're just a friend. Anything more would be too weird."

"Okay, okay. Let's just eat and then I'll take you home?"

I looked at him for a moment and nodded.

Britnee had brought us a platter of chicken fingers, celery, hot wings, fries, and potato boats. I knew I needed to eat, so picked at a few things. I wasn't really hungry and just wished I was at home in bed. Alone. Feeling sorry for myself, I drank one more glass of champagne. The room was soon spinning and the music was pounding. Everett stood and pulled me out of the booth, dragging me onto the dance floor. I tried to pull away from him, but risked falling over.

He held me close to him in stark contrast to other couples who were moving in a fast rhythm to the music. I never had understood these kinds of places or why people liked to fling their bodies around. I also knew I was the quiet wallflower who would never fit in with people like those who surrounded me. I wondered how many of them had faced death before. I closed my eyes as Everett put a hand on my back and pressed himself closer to me, slow-dancing to a very loud and fast song. I knew I needed to back away from him, as to not give him the wrong idea, but for a moment I felt grounded and almost able to forget about the sights, sounds, and smells from the day before. Soon I felt his cheek close to my own and his warm breath on my neck.

The song ended, and in the brief moment of silence before the next began, he whispered into my ear.

"Hat, please. Give me a chance."

As his lips brushed against my own, I placed my palms against his chest and attempted to push him away.

"Stop, Everett. You're drunk."

He pulled me back to him and attempted to resume the kiss that had not really even begun. I tried to push him away a second time, but he was too strong. He held me so tightly that it hurt, causing me to wince. As his tongue began to force its way into my mouth, we were suddenly separated. Everett was pushed backward, a couple of feet away from me. A man stood with his back to me, facing Everett. He was tall with dark hair, blue jeans, and a tight white t-shirt.

"I believe the lady said no," said a deep voice that was somewhat familiar.

"Fuck off," said Everett, who was taking a step toward the man who had just addressed him. "It's between me and her."

"Not tonight, man. Hattie said no."

I wondered how he knew my name. My question was answered when he turned to face me. My heart skipped a beat, seeing the one face I had longed to see since the day prior.

"Saul…"

"You know this asshole, Hattie?" asked Everett.

"Yes she does," answered Saul. "We go way back. Hattie, you ready to leave?"

I just nodded at him.

"Do you have a jacket?"

I shook my head no.

"Hattie, I promised your brother I'd take you home," mumbled Everett.

Saul enveloped my hand in his. He gently led me toward the stairs, and I went willingly.

"You can explain later," he whispered. "Let's just get you out of here."

CHAPTER 6 ~ COMING UP FOR AIR

I felt Everett's eyes on me the entire walk up the stairway. I knew he was pissed, but he had no right to try to force a relationship. Saul kept my hand in his. We walked through the pig-decorated upper portion of the pub and finally slipped outside into the cool night air.

"It's dark out," I muttered. I had lost track of time.

"Hattie, who was that?"

"Everett. A friend of my brother's. Well, a friend of ours. We all went to school together."

"He looked like he was getting a bit too friendly with you."

"Yeah. He thinks we should fall in love. What are you doing here?" I asked, changing the subject.

"I was meeting a friend for a drink. He canceled at the last minute."

"A boyfriend?"

Saul laughed deeply. "No, Hattie. A potential business partner."

"Oh."

"I'm not gay," he said in a very serious voice.

"Me either."

"How much have you had to drink?"

I shrugged. "Maybe four or five?"

"I'll take you home if that's okay?"

"I don't want to go home."

"You should sleep it off."

I shook my head side to side. "Every time I close my eyes, I see the fire. I hear all those people screaming."

Saul rubbed at his chin with his fingers. His five-o-clock shadow was rugged looking, and quite sexy. "You can come home with me if you want. I'll make you some coffee. We can talk about what happened yesterday."

I looked down, realizing we were still holding hands. "You sure you don't mind?"

"I'm sure. But didn't your mother tell you not to talk to strangers, or go to their homes?"

"She died when I was born."

"Crap. I'm sorry, Hattie."

I shrugged. "It's ok. I don't remember her. Besides, you're not a stranger. You saved my life."

"Let's get you out of here and sobered up."

"Wait...Everett...he shouldn't drive."

"Don't worry. I'll call the staff. They'll call him a cab."

"You sure?"

"Positive. C'mon, let's get out of here."

He kept my hand in his and walked me down the sidewalk toward his truck.

"Hattie!" I heard Everett yelling from behind us. "Hattie, you can't just go off with some dude!"

I felt Saul squeeze my hand as he slowed to a stop and turned to face my long-time-friend-turned-jerk-for-the-night.

"Leave it be, man" said Saul in his husky voice.

"No way, Dude. I don't know you and Hattie's not going off with some fucking guy I don't know."

47

Everett was slowly approaching us. By his facial expression I could tell he was really pissed. Saul must have sensed it too, because he put an arm out in front of me to keep himself between me and Everett.

"Back off, man," said Saul. "I really don't want to hurt you, but I will."

I had a feeling this might end badly. I stepped to the side so that I was still behind Saul, but so that Everett could see me.

"Everett. Take a cab home, ok? I'll see you tomorrow and I promise we'll talk."

"This is horseshit, Hat. If this fucker hurts a single hair on your head Joe and I will both kill him."

"Go home, Ev. Just go home," I said as I found Saul's hand again and slowly pulled him toward his truck. I didn't look back at Everett.

***

I sat quietly beside Saul, trying to not shiver. It was a cold night and even though he'd turned the heater on, it hadn't warmed the cab yet.

"I'd offer you a jacket, but you took it home with you," he said quietly.

"I'll be okay."

"It'll warm up soon."

The drive to Saul's cabin only took about twenty minutes. He was kind enough to not ask any questions about me and Everett. Once we were there, we were greeted with a welcome quietness; the gentle lapping of waves nearby, the barking of a sea lion in the distance, but otherwise just *quiet*.

As Saul unlocked the ivy-draped front door, he looked at me sideways.

"You ever go fishing, Hattie?"

"Nope."

"Maybe I'll take you."

He held the door open for me and I stepped into a dimly lit living room. He had left a single lamp on beside a big overstuffed couch that was covered in dark plaid fabric. Despite the ambient temperature being cool, the room was warm and inviting.

"Go ahead and sit down. I'll light a fire and get it warmed up in here."

"Thanks."

"Sorry the fireplace is the only way to get heat around here."

There was a split-log chair with similar fabric as the couch, but it didn't look very comfortable. I opted to occupy one end of the sofa. I sat back and slumped against the armrest, making myself comfortable.

Saul knelt down in front of an older-looking wood stove and began crinkling newspaper and inserting small pieces of kindling. Before long the fire was crackling and he added a couple of larger logs. Once it was burning on its own, he turned and walked toward me.

"Alright, Hattie. You ready to talk?"

I looked at him with dread. "About what?"

"Anything you want. How about I make some coffee?"

"Do you have any tea?"

He grinned at me, the gesture lighting up his whole face. "Yes, I have tea. Herbal or black?"

"Black, with two sugars?"

"Hang tight and I'll be right back with it."

I watched as he left the room through an open archway that I assumed led to a kitchen. I only saw two other doorways, which I imagined were a bedroom and bathroom. The walls were all made of logs. I had never been in a real log cabin before. I stared at an animal head mounted on the wall, wondering if it was a deer or an elk. My feet were aching, so I slipped my sandals off and curled my feet under my butt. I allowed myself to sink into the couch, curling up in an attempt to get warm. My stomach was sour and my head was starting to ache from too much alcohol.

After several minutes, Saul walked back through the archway, carrying two steaming mugs. I sat up straighter and took the mug he held out for me.

"Careful, it's hot."

"Thanks," I whispered.

"It's just Lipton. I hope that's ok?"

"It's perfect."

I sipped on it carefully, avoiding burning my lips.

"Is it sweet enough?"

I nodded.

Saul sat beside me, in the middle seat. My heart skipped a little beat at him opting for such a close position. I noticed he had taken his shoes and socks off, too. He had big feet with long toes. Like the rest of him, they looked strong.

"Did you want to talk about what happened tonight?" he asked me.

"My brother got married," I explained. "They wanted to go out for drinks afterward."

"So you know that guy well?"

"Everett?" I asked, immediately taking another sip of tea.

Saul nodded.

"Yeah. I've known him since my brother Joe and I were in kindergarten."

"You guys went to kindergarten together, all three of you?"

I nodded. "Joe's my twin. We grew up doing pretty much everything together. The Fidalgo Bay elementary school was small enough to force us to be in the same classes all the way till middle school."

"Ok, so this friend of yours, Everett, all of a sudden he wants to date you? Or has this been going on for a while?"

I shook my head. "He's kind of always had a thing for me, but we've never dated. He's more like an older brother. We even talked about it after you dropped me off at home last night. He and his mom stayed over and I couldn't sleep. I explained that I just didn't feel that way about him. Then he pulled this crap tonight."

"Well, I suppose I can't fault him for being attracted to a pretty girl, but no means no. He crossed a line."

I felt my face flush at the compliment he had snuck in.

"So, tell me about you," I suggested.

"What do you want to know?"

"Well, anything I suppose. What are you doing living here?"

"My grandfather passed away about a year ago. The rest of the family fought over his estate, but he left everything, including this place, to me and my little sister. It's not much, but I used to stay here with him a few weeks every summer. It was pretty special to us."

"I'm sorry he passed."

He bowed his head for a moment. Looking up again, he quietly said "thanks."

"Do you think you'll stay here?"

"I imagine so. I left my job back in the city. Came here with a little savings. I imagine I'll look for a job soon."

"What kind of work?"

"Probably construction. Maybe dock work or fishing. I like to be outside."

I yawned.

"Am I boring you?"

I shook my head no and chuckled. "No. Sorry."

"So, why were you drinking so much tonight?"

I leaned my head back, resting it on the back of the couch. "I just wanted to feel numb for a while. Try to forget about the explosions."

"It's gonna take time."

"I feel like a freak. It's hard to sleep, eat…think. All those people who died. Their screams. Bodies in the street. That baby…and its mother…"

I could feel a hot tear fall down my cheek. The last thing I wanted to do was cry in front of this man that I barely knew. Before I had a chance to wipe it away, I felt the heat of his hand doing it for me. Before I knew it, I was in his arms, crying into his chest.

"It's ok, let it out. Just let it out," he soothed.

I had never been comfortable with people seeing me cry, and I had never really been close enough to anyone to cry against them before.

"I'm sorry," I mumbled.

He rubbed at my back gently with one hand, the other smoothing my hair. "Shhh, it's fine."

I forced myself to stop crying and moved back from him enough to wipe my eyes. Again, Saul took over with his thumbs and gently wiped the tears away from beneath my eyes. He was looking at me with a softness that warmed me.

"It's pretty incredible," he whispered.

I looked at him questioningly.

"How beautiful you are, even when you're crying," he said softly.

I wiped a stray tear from my neck. "I am not."

"I'm glad I saved you, Hattie."

I felt my face warm under his stare.

"I think you have a lot to offer this world," he continued.

"You're embarrassing me," I admitted.

"I'm sorry. I didn't mean to." He paused. "Come fishing with me tomorrow?"

I looked at him, unsure. "Okay."

He smiled, showing off his straight white teeth. They were almost too perfect. "Good."

"Did you have braces when you were younger?" I asked.

He laughed at the question. "Yup, sure did. Let's go to bed."

My eyes must have widened because he laughed again.

"I'm not that kind of guy. I think you're gorgeous, Hattie. And I love your personality. Maybe someday I'll get a chance with you, but tonight you can have my bed. I'll take the couch."

I smiled awkwardly.

"You're not used to compliments, are you?"

I shook my head back and forth.

Saul stood, offering me his hand. I took it, a bit unsure. I knew so little about this man yet trusted him with my life. He led me through one of the closed doors, into a small bedroom with a bed covered in a heavy wool blanket in shades of blue, green, and yellow. There was a dresser next to the door and a simple wood night stand beside the bed. Saul walked to the dresser and pulled out a t-shirt.

"Here. You can borrow this."

"Thanks. It'll be a lot more comfortable than my dress."

He opened a different drawer and pulled out a pair of sweat-pant shorts. "These'll be too big for you but they have a drawstring."

"Is there anything else you need?"

"Maybe just the bathroom?"

"Yes, I have one of those," he said with a wink. It made me smile.

CHAPTER 7 ~ NIGHTMARES

After a quick shower and change of clothes, I emerged from the bathroom to find Saul arranging his makeshift bed on the couch.

"Feel better?" he asked.

I nodded. "Yes. Thanks for the shower and clothes."

He walked over to me and ran a hand over my hair. "Your hair's wet."

"I didn't see a hair drier. Don't worry, it'll dry."

Something about the way he was looking into my eyes made my stomach flip-flop and tingle. His hand was still on the side of my head, cupping it gently. He was standing so close that I could feel his body heat radiating. Without realizing what I was doing, I closed my eyes and leaned into his palm. I could hear his breathing slow and deepen and sensed his face close to my own. Surreally, the heat of his soft lips set me on fire as he kissed me tenderly. His fingers wound through my damp hair as he deepened the kiss, tasting me sweetly. I returned his advance, opening my mouth to accept his affection. I wasn't even sure if I was doing it right since I had only ever kissed one boy on the lips before: Fred Malloy in ninth grade. I felt weak in the knees as if the world had fallen away from me. I breathed in through my nose, inhaling his manly scent while tasting his mouth. Saul groaned into my mouth, and suddenly broke the kiss.

"Slow down, girl." He was slightly out of breath.

"I'm sorry," I muttered, not sure what else to say.

He laughed, making my face darken to what must have been seven shades of red.

"Hattie, I kissed you. You have nothing to apologize for. I just know you've been drinking, and I don't want to move too fast." He sighed heavily. "Ok, so I want to, but I won't. You need to know I have genuine respect for you."

I must have pouted, because he took one hand and cupped my chin, forcing me to look at him. If you want to explore things between us once you're sober, we can. But there's no rush. Really."

I thought for a moment. "Well, was it any good?"

He chuckled again. "The kiss?"

I nodded silently, still feeling flushed.

"Yes. More than good."

"I wasn't sure if I was doing it right."

He looked at me slightly confused, and slightly horrified. "Hattie? That was your first kiss?"

I bit my lip nervously. "Well, a guy dry kissed me on the lips in high school. Does that count?"

He didn't laugh this time. He just shook his head slowly from side to side. "No, that doesn't count."

"Sorry."

"Stop apologizing."

He set his forehead against my own and cupped the base of my head in his hand, causing my heart to beat faster. My head was spinning.

"You need to get some sleep. We'll talk in the morning, okay?"

I nodded.

"Leave the bedroom door open so you get the heat from the fireplace. It'll dry that pretty hair of yours."

I nodded again. He let go of me and placed his hands on my shoulders, turning me around to face the bedroom. "Sweet dreams, sweet Hattie."

I shuffled forward, not daring to look back at him. I climbed onto his bed and slid under the covers. The sheets smelled like fabric softener. I welcomed the softness of the mattress and pillows. It felt almost like a long awaited hug. As I drifted off to sleep, I found myself wishing that Saul was beside me.

***

It was a sunny day and I was walking with a bouquet of daisies in my hands. I was barefoot and wearing a sheer blue sundress that tickled my ankles as I walked. A breeze carried in the calls of seagulls and the musty scent of low tide. There was something wrong with the sky. The color was off. It should have been a warm yellow glow from the midday sun. Instead, it was the deep color of glowing embers. It made everything look an awkward shade of pink-orange and was starting to hurt my eyes. Looking down at the flowers in my hands, I realized they were now scorched and blackened. They crumbled in my hands, falling to the ground at my feet in a small pile of ash that was quickly carried away by the wind. The wind. It had gotten stronger and was blowing hot against my face. I began to run, my bare feet burning on the sidewalk. People were slowly walking toward me. As each passed, they mouthed "it should have been you." I looked back and saw them fade into nothing. I knew they were dead.

A baby began crying hysterically. It sounded like it was crying from pain. I looked around, but all I could see were flames. The heat was growing intolerable. The crying was so loud that my ears were hurting. The cries changed to a woman calling out for her baby. Suddenly she was standing in front of me. Her mouth was opening as if she were screaming, but there was only the constant crackle of fire. Without hearing her words, I knew she was screaming at me for taking her baby.

"Hattie, wake up."

The room was dark. I wasn't sure where I was. Something was wrong. It was hard to breathe and my chest felt tight.

"We have to help them," I choked out.

"Hattie. It's Saul. You're ok."

I sat upright in the bed, trying to catch my breath.

"It's so hot," I moaned as I tried to kick off the covers.

"I think you had a bad dream. You were trying to yell out in your sleep."

"The baby's mom was looking for it. And the people who died…"

"Shhh. It's over now."

"They told me I should have been the one to die," I said as I tried to breathe.

My eyes were adjusting to the dark and Saul looked like an angel with the faint glow of the firelight behind him.

"I should have died instead," I said in a hoarse whisper.

"No. It wasn't your time," he said softly.

He wrapped his strong arms around me and held me, soothing me by rubbing my back gently.

"It was so real," I mumbled into his neck. "I could feel the heat from the fire burning me."

"You're okay now. I won't let anything hurt you."

"I'm sorry I woke you up," I said sincerely.

"Don't be," he whispered. His voice had deepened noticeably.

He unwrapped his arms from around me and placed a palm on each side of my face, forcing me to look at him.

"I want to be here for you, Hattie. Okay?"

I couldn't nod my head with the way he was holding me, so just looked into his eyes. He leaned forward, hesitating with his lips close enough to mine to feel the heat, as if asking for permission. When I didn't back away, he continued forward until his lips parted mine softly. He kissed me gently but with a passion that was stronger than our first kiss only hours before. He was so tender with me that it nearly brought tears to my eyes.

He slowly let go of my face and moved his hands down my arms, never moving his lips from mine. His fingers ran down my upper arms slowly and lightly, sending little shivers through my skin. I closed my eyes and let myself relax under his touch. Every place his fingertips trailed was both hot and cold at the same time. I caught myself moaning softly into his mouth as he awoke desires deep within me.

He gently broke the kiss and I sighed.

"Was that okay?" he asked in a deep voice that hinted at longing.

I took a moment to breathe, not quite sure how to put into words just how okay it had been. He had stirred something inside of me that I had never felt before.

"Do you want me to stop?"

"No," I said, sounding a bit too desperate.

He almost instantly returned his lips to mine. My head was spinning as I felt the warmth of his hand beneath my t-shirt. His kiss was slow and tender, yet filled with need and want. He smelled of wood smoke and some sort of spice and his kiss tasted like vanilla and mint. I wrapped my arms around his back. He wasn't wearing a shirt and his skin was warm and smooth. He melted under my touch and groaned slightly. I felt a tingling sensation deep in my core and had trouble keeping my composure as his hands slid around to my front and gently stroked at my breasts. He moved his mouth down to my neck, which he sucked on gently at first. The sensation of him tasting my flesh caused me to groan deeply and knead the skin of his back, which in turn caused him to suck harder. He used his fingers to twist gently at my left nipple, leaving me quivering and I cried out softly.

His mouth left my neck and he kissed my cheek sweetly, very near to my ear. "Does it feel good?" he asked, whispering sweetly.

"Yes," I admitted.

"Good," he answered as his hands left the confines of my shirt. "But we need to stop now."

"No," I begged. "Please?"

He chuckled, almost evilly. "Hattie, seriously, I want to keep going but it's not the right time."

I heard an unusual noise of frustration escape my own lips and he chuckled again.

He followed my own protest with a sigh of his own. "You'll wake up hating me if we do this now. We barely know each other."

I didn't say anything. My feelings were a little hurt and I was being left very unsatisfied. To top it off, I still felt like I should have died in the explosion. To my horror, tears began welling in my eyes. I looked down at my lap, hoping he wouldn't notice.

"Oh, God, no. Don't cry," he said in dismay.

I tried as hard as I could, but my chin began quivering and I sniffled. I felt his hand under my chin and looked up as he gently lifted my face toward his. I could feel tears roll down my cheeks, despite trying so hard to keep them at bay. He took his thumbs and gracefully wiped the moisture from my face, and followed with tiny little kisses down each cheek.

"Can you at least hold me for a while?" I choked out in a pathetically broken voice. I had always had a difficult time speaking when crying.

He wrapped his arms around me and held me tight. I leaned into the crook of his neck and inhaled. His scent was almost as calming as his touch.

"You should try to get some more sleep," he said next to my head.

"Stay with me?"

I felt like a child asking, but being alone was the last thing I wanted. He let go of me and looked me in the eyes.

"I won't go anywhere, I promise."

I nodded.

"Climb under the covers. It's cold in here."

I did as instructed, settling back down in the bed. I felt Saul climb under the covers behind me. He wrapped an arm across me and held me close.

"Sleep," he whispered.

I closed my eyes and tried to tune out all of the thoughts swimming through my head. Saul's hand slowly moved down and settled just below my belly button. It caused me to squirm slightly, which in turn caused Saul to reposition himself a bit. I wriggled under his arm until I was able to turn and face him. The fire in the other room was dying down, and the light in the bedroom was nearly gone.

"Hey," he whispered.

"Hey."

I reached one of my hands out from under the covers and placed it on his bare chest.

"Saul?"

"Hmm?"

"I feel like I've known you for a long time."

He took my hand in his and wove his fingers through my own.

"I know what you mean," he said. "And I think I'd like to know you for a long time."

I snuggled up close to him and fell asleep in his arms.

CHAPTER 8 ~ SUNSHINE AND HONEY

I woke not knowing where I was. Blinking my eyes, I sat up in bed and saw that the room I was in was full of dark shades of brown and orange and red. Saul. I was in Saul's room. Remembering falling asleep with him, my heart started racing when I realized I was now alone. I gripped the sheets with my hands and took a deep breath, willing myself to calm down. It wasn't like me to feel anxious like this. I swung my legs out from under the covers and slid out of the bed until my feet touched the floor. There was a thick wool area rug covering a portion of the wood floor. I walked toward the bathroom. Once my feet left the rug, the chill of the room hit me head-on. I rushed the rest of the distance to the bathroom door. Once inside, I stared at myself in the mirror. My hair was a mess and I looked scrawny in Saul's large t-shirt. It had a chipmunk on the front, which made me giggle to myself. I hurried and used the toilet, and then returned to the mirror. I felt guilty doing so, but decided to search the two drawers in the cabinet in front of me. I had hoped for a brush, but had to settle for a comb. I tamed my curls the best I could and then braided my hair over my left shoulder. I didn't have a hair tie or rubber band, so knew it wouldn't last long. I found a tube of Crest and put some on my index finger, which I used to scrub my teeth.

Walking back into the bedroom, I looked around for the sweatpant shorts Saul had loaned me. Coming up empty, I decided to be brave and left the bedroom wearing just the t-shirt and my panties. The rest of the cabin smelled of bacon and cinnamon rolls. My stomach began growling. Saul was standing in the kitchen, wearing the missing sweats he had let me borrow but still bare-chested. He looked up, smiling, as I approached. He was even hotter than I had recalled and I knew I was blushing.

"Morning," he said with a quick wink.

"Morning." I stood in the middle of the room, just watching him. I wasn't sure really how to act, and felt a bit vulnerable wearing what I was.

"Hungry?" he asked.

I nodded.

"Bacon will be ready in about two minutes. Cinnamon rolls are still on the table. OJ's fresh." He chuckled. "Ok, well, the OJ is from a bottle."

I walked slowly toward him, holding the hem of the t-shirt down a bit. He watched me like he wanted to eat me for dessert, making my face feel even warmer. He began piling the sizzling bacon onto a plate that was lined with a paper towel, and carried it to a small dinette set where a plate of scrambled eggs and cinnamon rolls waited.

"Sorry the chairs don't match," he said with a smile. "Not much in this place does."

"That's okay."

I sat in one of the two chairs and stretched the t-shirt over my knees.

He placed two strips of bacon onto my plate and followed it with a scoop of eggs and a cinnamon roll. I wasn't used to being waited upon.

"Thanks, Saul. This was really nice of you."

He sat across from me and piled food onto his own plate. I took a bite of eggs first.

"Like them?" he asked, scooping a bite of eggs into his own mouth.

"Mmm hmm."

"I use onion salt. Just a pinch. I'm famous for my eggs."

"They're good."

"Just good?" he faked surprise.

"Well..." I began. "I've had better."

I took another bite and watched his face.

"Better than these? When?"

"Last night."

I smiled when he looked confused.

"You, Saul. You tasted better." I rolled my eyes at him teasingly.

Slowly, a grin spread across his face.

"You ready to go fishing today?"

I nodded. "Yeah, but I need some clothes."

"Nah, you look great just like you are. Especially blushing like that."

"Sorry about that. I've always gotten embarrassed easily. My face will turn fifty shades of red if I'm not careful."

"Do you want to call home? Let them know you're okay?"

I shook my head. "Maybe later."

"They're probably worried."

"I know. After breakfast?"

He sighed gently. "Okay."

We continued to eat in relative silence, occasionally sneaking a quick glance at one another. I wasn't able to finish all of my food, but Saul was glad to help. He ate more than anyone I had ever seen before. He caught me smiling at him and winked at me.

***

We spent the rest of the morning sitting on the couch in his living room, watching the fire. It was the most relaxed I'd been in days. We talked about silly things: what we had wanted to be when we grew up, our favorite bands and colors and foods. He was easy to be around, despite my inexperience with men.

"Are we really going fishing today?" I asked.

"If you want to, sure. I have a little rowboat and two poles. All we'd need is bait. Oh, and fishing licenses. We'll grab you one in town. Some clothes too. Actually, it's close to noon. We should get going."

I nodded. My legs were draped over his lap and I lifted them, swinging them over the edge of the couch. He stood and offered me a free hand, which I took all too willingly. His hand was big, and his fingers long. My own small hand became lost in his grip.

"You have tiny hands," he said.

I smiled. "I was just thinking about how big yours are."

"They can do magical things," he said with a smug grin. "Maybe I'll show you later."

I wasn't quite sure how to take what he had said, and my face must have showed my surprise.

"Get your mind out of the gutter. I was just talking about a back rub."

He stood facing me, now holding both of my hands in his. I didn't really see him step closer, but all of a sudden he was so near that I could feel his body heat. He leaned down and kissed the middle of my forehead.

"You need to call home," he whispered.

I groaned. It hadn't been quite what I had wanted to hear. "Yeah. I guess so."

Saul reached behind himself and took his cell phone off of the coffee table. "I can wait in the other room if you want?" he offered as he handed me the smartphone.

I shook my head 'no' and began to dial. I knew no one would be home, but dialed our landline first anyway. To my surprise, the line was answered on the first ring.

"Hello?" It was Justine's voice.

"Justine? It's Hattie."

"Hattie! My God! We're all so worried. Where are you?"

"I'm ok. I'm with a friend."

I could hear Joe yelling in the background, demanding the phone.

I sat on the couch, waiting for Justine to say something. Anything.

"Justine?"

"Hat. It's Joe. Where they hell are you? I'll come get you."

"Joe. Calm down. I'm fine."

I was met with silence, other than people in the background asking what was going on and if I was okay. I could picture Joe with his nervous habit of grabbing his hair in his fist while he thought.

"Hattie. You've had us all scared shitless. Tell me where you are and I'll come get you."

I could tell by his tone that he was pissed.

"Joe, I'm fine. My friend will bring me home later."

"You mean that fucking stranger Everett saw you leave the club with?"

"He's not a stranger. And stop talking to me like that."

"C'mon, this is ridiculous. You've already ruined our wedding night, Hattie. We're all worried about you."

"Well, I guess you can thank Everett for that."

I was getting angry and trying to not hang up on him.

Saul held his hand out for the phone, obviously picking up on my frustration. "I'll talk to him," he said.

"Hang on, Joe."

I handed the phone to Saul and leaned back against the couch cushions

"Saul here. Yes, she's fine. She's not quite ready yet but I'll have her home tonight."

I took a deep breath. I had no idea everyone had been sitting around worried about me.

"Uh huh," continued Saul. "She's fine, I promise. And I'll keep her that way."

Saul took the phone from his ear and handed it back to me.

"Someone named Miranda wants to talk to you."

I sighed, and then held the phone to my ear. "Hi Miranda."

"Hattie, can you please just let one of us come get you?"

"I'll be home later."

Her pause worried me. "You just stay safe, you hear?"

"I am. I will. Bye."

I hit the end button on the phone and handed it back to Saul.

"They sound pretty pissed," he said.

"Yeah. I guess so."

"You sure you don't want me to take you back? You can show them you're okay and I can pick you up later. We could fish another day, and you could let me take you out to dinner tonight instead?"

"I guess I do need some clothes. I can't live in your t-shirt."

He grinned, showing off his awesome smile. "You could live out of it."

I leaned back and nudged him lightly with a bare foot.

"Okay. You win. You can take me home, but will you pick me up by two o'clock? I have a feeling I won't want to be there for long."

"That I can do. Even better, we'll stop and get you a prepaid cell. That way you can call me if you need me."

"Why are you being so nice to me?" I stretched my legs out and put them on his lap. He rubbed my bare shins, warming me.

"Because I really like you."

He looked at me unsmiling, his eyes bright and his face full of sincerity. I smiled softly in return, and reached a hand out toward him. He took it and we connected on a level that was quiet and soft.

"I like you too, Saul."

He held his other arm out, indicating he wanted me to come closer. I moved my legs from his lap and tucked them behind me and then scooted closer to him. I had intended to just lean against his side, but he wrapped his arms around me and moved me onto his lap. I leaned against his bare chest as his strong arms held me tight. I felt his lips kiss the top of my head and I snuggled closer.

"You smell good," he whispered. "Like sunshine and honey."

I could feel a hardness in his lap.

"What's wrong?" he asked, sensing me tense.

"Uh…" I was a bit too embarrassed to explain that I could feel his manhood.

"Hattie, you're on your sixth shade of red. What is it?" He looked genuinely concerned.

I started to get off his lap but he kept a hold on me.

"Ah, sorry about that," he said, finally realizing what was wrong. "It has a mind of its own."

I looked away, somewhat mortified and really not sure how to handle the situation. All I had wanted during the night was to explore his body and vice versa, but now, fully awake, I suddenly felt self-conscious.

"Hey, it's all right. I swear I'll keep it in my pants and make it behave."

He began laughing, and I knew by how hot my face felt that it must be my awkwardness that he found funny.

"Oh my God this is embarrassing," I groaned.

"Hattie. Look at me." His voice was deep, soothing, and very serious.

I looked at his chest, and he placed a finger under my chin to encourage me to meet his eyes.

"That's better," he said quietly.

We just looked at each other for a long moment. As the silence grew awkward, I acted without much thought. I leaned forward and placed my lips upon his. I had hoped he'd take it from there, but I felt his body tense and he didn't kiss me back quite like I had expected. I backed away just far enough to look him in the eyes again. His face had a softness about it, and his eyes were full of longing in contrast to his lack of response to my feeble attempt at romance. He was breathing deeply and slowly. I placed a palm against his chest and slowly moved my legs so that I was straddling him. His lap was still telling me he was interested, as were his eyes. I felt the rise and fall of his chest with my hand, and gently placed the other on the side of his face. His face was rugged, and his stubble unexpectedly soft.

I leaned forward again, kissing him on the lips a bit more firmly. As I tasted him and inhaled his scent, he finally responded as I had craved. Together we deepened the kiss, our mouths hungrily taking each other in.

He slowly moved his mouth from mine, trailing his tongue down the side of my neck to my ear. "Are you sure you want this?"

I leaned back a bit, nodding softly. He took hold of the bottom of the t-shirt I was wearing, and gently lifted it upward. I raised my arms as he pulled it over my head. I had never sat naked in front of a man before, and swallowed hard in fear that he might hate what he saw.

"You're beautiful," he said with a soft sigh.

He placed his large hands over my bare breasts, kneading them gently and lovingly. I bit my lower lip and closed my eyes. My body began to take over and I ground myself against the bulge in his pants.

"Oh good God," moaned Saul just before he was back to kissing me deeply.

Suddenly he stood, with me still on his front. I wrapped my legs around him as he carried me to the bedroom. Suddenly I was lying on my back on his bed, and he was on top of me. Supporting his weight on one arm, he looked down at me.

"We shouldn't do this, not yet," he said, making sure I was listening.

"I need to feel you," was all I could manage to whisper.

He leaned down again, kissing me passionately. Eventually his lips moved down my neck and when I felt his hot mouth encircle one of my breasts and begin sucking on my erect nipple I arched my back and fought to breathe. His hand slid down my bare side and tugged at the side of my panties. I lifted my butt off of the bed and he slid them down my legs. He never faltered in his attempts to devour my breast as he slid my only remaining shred of clothing past my feet.

He moved his head down, using the tip of his tongue to trace a line from my breast to my belly button. As his mouth moved lower, I began gasping for air.

"Is this ok?" he asked while still working my flesh with his mouth.

"Uh huh."

He used his hands to gently part my legs, and again trailed his tongue lower until I could feel the hotness of his mouth on my most private of places. I moaned, louder than I had meant to. He groaned against me in response, taking my flesh into his mouth and sucking gently. When his hot tongue entered me, I cried out in a sharp whimper of pleasure. He continued to taste me, long and slow, and it drove me wild. When he stopped suddenly, I looked up to see what was wrong.

"Hattie, I have to stop."

"Why?" I asked, sounding like a pathetically sad child.

"Because if we don't, I don't think I'll be able to."

He climbed back up onto the bed with me, half laying on top of me. He pressed himself against me, his shorts still on but doing little to hide his intense desire.

"You have no idea how much I want to take it all the way, beautiful. I don't want your first time being rushed, or you leaving here feeling like it was a mistake."

"Saul, I'm sure. It's what I want. I can't explain it, but I need you. I feel like I've been looking for you my whole life."

He leaned down and kissed me with deep passion, his hand exploring my side. Without words, he was telling me that he felt the same way.

"I promise I'll be gentle, if you promise you won't regret it?"

I nodded. "No regrets. Ever."

"Okay. Just give me a sec while I grab a condom?"

My body felt like it was on fire with desire and the several seconds he was out of my reach were torture. Facing away from me, he slipped his sweat pants off and I watched as he stood there naked. His butt was firm, and his muscles alone were enough to make me squirm. I could hear him pull open a drawer from the dresser and heard a little foil package being torn open. I scooted myself up in the bed until my head was resting on a pillow. I watched as Saul fiddled with something out of my view and waited for him to walk back to me. The room was cold, so I grabbed the covers that were still messy from our night's sleep and covered myself. As he turned to face me, I swallowed hard. He was gorgeous; every inch of him.

He climbed into the bed beside me, slipping under the covers so he could feel me. His skin was smooth and warm and my body tingled in anticipation of his touch. He climbed halfway on top of me again, parting my legs with his own. I stroked his biceps gently, exploring his curves. He leaned down and whispered near my ear.

"I'll be gentle, baby, but let me know if you need me to slow down."

He looked at me with sincerity and waited for me to acknowledge him.

"I will."

He leaned down again, kissing me hard. He took my breath away and I tasted his desire as he slowly slid himself inside of me. Time seemed to stand still as he showed me pleasure that I had, until then, only heard stories about. In his arms, I forgot about the world around me. No thoughts of my family and friends being angry with me. No thoughts about the explosion. No thoughts about my father and his wife.

CHAPTER 9 ~ I'LL CALL YOU

We stayed in bed for another half an hour, quietly talking about random things. I discovered that Saul was deathly allergic to cherries and had a younger sister in Virginia, named Carolina, who he usually called Lina for short. She was the only relative he was still close to. I loved listening to his voice and feeling him next to me. Eventually he announced that it was time to 'head out' and face fears.

He searched his dresser and found a pair of exercise shorts that cinched at the waist with a tie, and tossed them to me.

I dressed quietly, sneaking peeks as he changed into a pair of jeans and a t-shirt. My hair was a disaster, so I borrowed a rubber band from Saul and tied it behind my head in something resembling a ponytail.

Like a gentleman, he opened the passenger door to his truck for me and I climbed in. I reluctantly buckled up, not wanting to leave the magic of the little seaside home. It was overcast and cool, and seagulls were circling in the air nearby. As Saul took his seat behind the wheel, I looked over at him and smiled awkwardly.

"I want to stop in town real quick if that's ok?" he asked.

"Sure. I'm in no hurry to get back. Oh. Do you mind if I wait in the car, though?"

"Why?"

I rolled my eyes at him teasingly. "Oh…let's see. My hair's a mess, you gave me a hickey, my clothes are like ten sizes too big, I'm not wearing a bra…"

"I gave you a hickey?" he asked, seemingly oblivious to his love mark.

I nodded slyly and turned my head to the side for him to see.

"Damn, sorry."

"It's okay. I kinda like it."

I grinned at him and he flashed me a smile as he started the truck and backed it up onto the road out front. The drive into town only took about ten minutes. Tide was low and the mud flats of Puget Sound fascinated me as always. I found myself lost in thought.

"Saul?"

"Yeah?"

"Are you still taking me out tonight?"

"You bet, if you're still willing to go?"

"What should I wear?"

"Casual tonight. And warm."

"Jeans ok?"

He looked me over slowly. "Anything on you I'm sure is great. If I'm lucky maybe you'll let me take your clothes off later."

I felt my face flush again.

Saul pulled into a parking spot in front of Radio Shack and left the engine running.

"Lock the doors while I'm inside, ok?"

"Sure."

"I won't be long."

"Okay."

He leaned across the cab and kissed me softly on the lips, and then just as suddenly was standing outside of the truck, closing the door. I pushed the lock button, as he had asked. I watched as he walked into the store.

Once he was out of sight, I turned on the radio and the cab was filled with classical music. I tried to change stations but quickly realized it was a CD. I hadn't figured Saul for a classical music kind-of guy.

After about fifteen minutes, he came back out holding a small plastic sack. I unlocked the doors for him and he slid back into his seat.

"Ah, you found my music."

I nodded. "It's soothing."

"Here, this is for you."

He handed me the bag, and I looked at it questioningly. I reached inside and pulled out a brand new iPhone. It was white with a pretty hard pink cover that had little half-pearls and clear sparkles in the shape of a daisy on the back.

"No, Saul, I can't take this."

I looked at him, afraid I'd hurt his feelings.

"That's okay. It's mine. You're just borrowing it."

"Saul!" I said, giving him a funny face.

"You need to be able to call me. I was due for an upgrade so just went ahead with a second line. It's really not a big deal."

"It's too much, really. A cheap flip-top would have been fine."

"Sure it would have. But they don't have pretty pink cases."

I frowned a bit, without really meaning to.

"C'mon. You lost yours in the explosion. Just let me do something nice for you, okay?"

I sighed and looked at him. "Okay. But I'll pay you back. And I'll only use it to call you."

"My number's programed in already. But it's unlimited talk, text, and data. Use it as much as you want, for whatever. Or whoever."

"You're really sweet, Saul. Thank you."

"Your e-mail is all set up too. I just used Outlook to create an account."

"You promise to answer if I call?"

"Of course. Always."

He started the engine and put a hand on my bare knee, giving it a quick squeeze before backing out of the parking spot.

"The charger's in the box in the bag. Make sure you plug it in as soon as you get home."

"What time are you picking me up?"

He looked at his watch. "It's almost twelve-thirty now. How about three o'clock?"

"Sounds good."

We listened to his CD for the rest of the trip, while I browsed through my new phone in a pretty pink case.

"Okay, we're here."

I looked up. The ride from the store to my house had gone by a lot faster than I had hoped. Joe's car was there in the driveway, with Miranda's parked next to it. I found myself greatly relieved to not see Everett's truck there. I made no effort to leave Saul's vehicle. I didn't feel like talking to anyone except for the man beside me, nor did I feel like explaining myself to anyone.

"You okay, sweet thing?"

I looked over at Saul and shrugged. "I guess I need to get it over with."

"Want me to come in with you?"

I forced a smile. "Yes, but I should deal with them alone."

"Is that guy here?"

"I don't see his truck."

"Okay. Try to get some rest. And just call if you need me."

I noticed the front door open. Joe was standing there; obviously irritated that he had to wait for me.

"That's your brother?"

"Yeah. Joe."

"He looks pissed."

"Yeah."

"Hattie?"

"Hmm?"

Saul looked at me intently. "I'll miss you."

He brought a genuine smile to my face. "Me too."

He leaned forward and kissed me. It felt almost like he was saying goodbye in a way I feared, and my heart skipped a beat.

"I'll be here at three o'clock," he whispered. He leaned his forehead against mine and gripped the back of my neck gently with one of his hands. "I'm not sure what spell you've cast, Hattie Leonardo, but you're turning my world upside down."

I reached up and grabbed his wrist and closed my eyes. For a moment I wished we were back in his tiny home, just the two of us.

"Promise me you'll come back?"

He kissed me again, harder than before. "I promise."

He let go of me. I made sure I had my new phone, and I slid out of the truck. I turned my back to the house and waved as Saul carefully pulled away from the curb.

I could sense Joe standing behind me, but kept facing the road until Saul's truck was gone from my sight. I already felt an emptiness within me.

"Hattie."

Joe's voice from behind me caused me to turn.

"We've all been worried, Hat. Are you okay?"

"I told you I'm fine," I said as I began to walk toward the house.

"That's all you have to say? You run off in the middle of the night with some guy you don't know and none of us knows why? You come home with a hickey on our neck and all you have to say is 'I told you I'm fine?'"

Almost to our porch, I stopped walking and whipped around to face him.

"Bullshit, Joe. Everett knows why I left with Saul."

"Saul? So the mystery guy's name is Saul? And what are you talking about Everett knows what?"

"What did Everett tell you?"

"That you got drunk after we left, some guy showed up saying he knew you, and you left. He said he begged you to stay."

"Joe. You know me. You've known me our whole lives. Everett got a little too demanding last night. He tried to kiss me and wouldn't stop when I said no."

Joe laughed at me, making me furious.

"It's not funny!"

"We've known Everett since we could barely walk, Hattie. He's not like that. He was probably just wasted."

"You did *not* just say that."

I turned and walked into the house, ignoring Miranda and Justine. I took the stairs two at a time and went to my bedroom, where I slammed the door before taking a couple of deep breaths to calm down. I could hear Joe downstairs, talking to the other women in a raised voice. Within moments all three were yelling, and it was clear they were all blaming me for overreacting. I set my pretty new phone on my dresser, stripped out of my borrowed clothes, wrapped myself in a bathrobe, and crossed the hall to the bathroom. Once inside, I locked the door and took an overly long shower. I was hoping everyone would be gone when I came out.

Once towel-dry, I put on a touch of make-up and lightly dried my hair. I decided to wear it down, but brushed it away from my face with a white cloth headband. To my relief, I didn't hear any more yelling from the main floor of the house. I put a simple pair of small silver hoops in my ears and headed back to my bedroom.

I could hear Miranda calling up for me as I slipped into pink lace panties and matching bra. I slid into a pair of faded blue jeans that I knew hugged my hips just right. I layered two tank tops, one lavender and one light blue, and threw on a lightweight white sweater, which I left open in front. I ignored Miranda and eventually she gave up on calling for me. A pair of white sandals left me ready to leave again. I looked at the clock and saw that it was only two o'clock. I checked myself in the full length mirror on the back of my door. My tanks were both low cut, the top one more so than the bottom, and I was pleased that just a touch of cleavage showed. Voices below began again. I picked out Justine's over the others. I really wished they'd all just leave. I picked my new cell up off the dresser and flopped onto my bed. I had forgotten to plug it in, so fished the charger from the bag and rolled onto my stomach so I could reach a nearby outlet. Once attached, the phone chirped and an image of Saul smiling at me came on the screen.

"Goofball," I said to myself.

I tuned out the sounds from the rest of the house and searched through the menu on the cell. I clicked the e-mail icon and smiled to myself when I saw that I had a message already.

To: Sunshine & Honey
From: Saul Meyers
Hi Hattie. I miss you. See you at 3:00. Saul.

I rolled onto my back, glad the charging cord was long enough. I hit the reply button and quickly typed a message back to him.

To: Saul Meyers
From: Sunshine & Honey
I miss you too. It's only 2:00. Wish it was 3. Yours, Hattie

I began to glance at other menu items, and sighed when I hear a knock on my door. I sat up, placing my phone on the bed beside me to charge.

"Who is it?" I called out softly.

"Miranda."

She went ahead and opened my door without waiting for my permission. Her eyes were red. She had obviously been crying.

"Hey," I said.

"Hey Sweetie. Can I sit?"

I nodded and patted the bed beside me.

"We were all really worried, Hat."

"I was fine, I promise."

"Okay. Can you promise me something, though?"

"Hmm?"

"If you're going to disappear, at least call me or Joe. Just let us know you're okay? You know I love you like you were my own."

I leaned against her and nodded. "I know. I just needed space. So much has happened the past couple days, Miranda. It feels like I can't breathe sometimes."

"You know I'm always here if you need to talk, right?"

"I know."

"Let's head downstairs? I'll make tea."

She stood, and I followed her lead. I grabbed my new phone and charger and headed downstairs. Joe and Justine were sitting on the loveseat together, holding hands. Neither said anything to me at first, for which I was glad. I walked to the end table that sat beside the larger sofa and plugged my phone in before sitting across from them.

"I'm sorry I worried you," I said apologetically.

"Hattie, if anything ever happened to you..." Joe's voice trailed off. "Just be careful, okay? Too much has happened."

I leaned my head back against the couch cushions and took a deep breath. Time was creeping by too slowly and I was starting to feel nervous about my date with Saul. After several long minutes of silence, Miranda came back into the room carrying two mugs of tea. She handed one to me, and one to Justine.

"Thanks," I said, truly grateful that this woman was trying to take care of me.

"Joe? Justine? Do you want to tell her?"

"Tell me what?" I asked.

Justine lifted her mug to her lips and blew on the steaming liquid to cool it. She smiled at me, and peeked sideways at Joe.

"We're having a baby," she said, grinning.

I looked at her for a moment, trying to comprehend her news.

"Serious?"

"In October," said Joe.

"Wow." I was speechless.

"Just 'wow?'" said Joe.

"Well, yeah, WOW," I repeated. "Congrats!" I smiled, the news finally sinking in. "A baby? Really?"

Justine giggled, and nodded as she sipped at her tea.

"Wow. Oh geez. Justine, I'm sorry I stressed you out." I suddenly felt horrible for causing her worry.

"Just don't do it again, okay?" she said with a smile.

I nodded. "As long as I get to babysit?"

She giggled again. "Sure you can!"

I sipped at my tea, trying to wrap my mind around their news. I looked up when there was a knock on the door.

I looked at my watch. 2:44.

"I'll get it," said Joe, standing.

I watched as he walked to the door. I choked on my tea when the door opened and it was my father and his wife Helen.

"Dad?" said Joe, obviously as surprised as I was.

"Joe. Good to see you, son."

Our father held his hand out to my brother, who took it and indulged him with a quick handshake.

"Helen," said Joe civilly.

"We came as soon as we heard about the explosion," said my father, still standing on the porch. "Where's Hattie?"

I stood, dreading talking to Helen. "Right here."

Helen pushed her way past Joe and into the living room.

"I told Jim we should just stay put and wait to hear from you. Why didn't you call?" she asked me condescendingly.

"Nice to see you too, Helen," I said in the prissiest voice I could manage.

"Have some respect Hattie," said my father. "We just flew in from across the globe to make sure you're okay."

"I'm fine, Jim," I said.

"Will you stop calling me that?"

I sighed. "Yes, Daddy."

Joe shut the door and my father and Helen sat on the couch.

"Can I get anyone a cup of tea?" asked Miranda.

"No. We won't be staying long, Manda," said my dad. They had been close when Joe and I were little kids and he had always called her that.

"At least stay for dinner? I know Hat's had a long day and Joe and Justine are tired. I'd be happy to cook."

"We need to check in to our hotel," chirped Helen. "How about if we all go out to dinner later?" She spoke in a soft Southern drawl and I had always suspected she faked it.

"Sounds good to me," said Justine.

"Sure," said Joe as he sat back down next to Justine. "We have a lot to talk about."

"By the way," said my father. "Congratulations to Mr. and Mrs. Leonardo!"

"Would have been nice if you'd have been here," I said, a bit too snippily.

"We're doing very important work in Kenya," said Helen. "I'm sure Joseph and Justine understand."

The room went quiet for a bit. I checked my watch again, and was thrilled to see it was nearly three o'clock. I checked my phone and was disappointed to not have any new messages. The charge was at ninety three percent, so I coiled the charger cord up and slipped it into my small handbag.

"New phone?" asked Justine.

I nodded. "My old one was in Joe's car when the explosion happened."

"Looks expensive," said Helen.

I just shrugged, not bothering to answer her, let alone look up at her.

"Well, it's three o'clock. We should go check in at the hotel. How about if we meet in Anacortes at four-thirty? At Myrtle's Steak House?" suggested my father.

"Steak sounds so good," said Justine. She sounded a bit too excited.

"Sure. We'll be there," said Joe.

"I'll let you guys have a nice family night," offered Miranda.

"No, Manda. Come. You know you're part of the family."

"He's right," said Helen. "You have to come." She didn't sound very convincing.

Miranda smiled. "If you insist."

"Hat? We can drive you," said Justine.

I had been picking at a loose thread on my jeans, but looked up. "Oh, I can't make it. Sorry."

My father stood. "We just flew in. It took us over thirty hours with layovers. Thousands of dollars for day-of tickets. You can meet us for dinner."

I clicked my phone on, glad to see Saul smiling at me, and was sad to see the clock read 3:07.

"I can't. I have plans already."

"Hattie, come on," said Justine. "It'll be fun."

I looked up. "I'm sure it'll be a whole heap…but I have plans already. Sorry."

Another knock sounded on the door, and I jumped up to answer it.

"C'mon, Jim, we need to get going," said Helen in her irritating nasal drawl.

The door opened on its own, and my heart sank when I saw Everett coming into my house. I had hoped it was Saul coming to pick me up, and Everett was the last person I wanted to see. Well, other than Helen.

"Hey honey," said Miranda. "Look who's here!"

"Mr. Leonardo. Mrs. Leonardo," he said, offering each of them his hand to shake. He had always known how to be a kiss-ass, and was in full charm mode.

***

Irritated beyond belief, I snuck out of the room while greetings were going around. I took my mug into the kitchen and felt sick to my stomach when I heard Everett's voice from behind me.

"Hattie?"

I turned to look at him but didn't answer.

"Can we talk? Please?"

"I'd rather not."

I turned to face the sink and rinsed my mug. I felt Everett standing close behind me, and held my breath. I didn't want him near me.

"I'm sorry, Hat," he whispered a little too close to the back of my head. "I didn't mean to freak you out. I had too much to drink and lost a little control."

I turned to face him, only to find he was even closer than I had anticipated. His front was nearly touching mine, forcing me to back against the counter.

"I guess you know now, huh?"

"Know what?" I asked.

"How I feel about you, Hat. I guess I've known for a while, but it didn't really slap me in the face until I thought you might have died in the explosion. I'm not sure what I would have done," he said, obviously on the verge of tears.

"Everett, stop. I didn't die. I'm flattered that you care about me, but what happened last night wasn't okay."

"I know, and I'm so sorry. If I could undo it I would, but I need you to know how I feel about you. And I want you to know that last night…well…it'll never happen again."

I didn't say anything at first, I just looked at him. He wore a mask of pain on his face, and in that moment I felt bad for him.

"Ev, you know I care about you too. We've been friends since we were just little. But that's what it is: a friendship. I don't want you hurting, and I'm not trying to be mean, but I only love you as a dear friend."

He stepped back from me a half turn, leaning against the counter that branched off into an 'L' shape. "You don't think it could ever be more?"

I looked sideways at him. "I just don't feel it, Ev."

"Can you at least forgive me for last night?"

"Yeah, I can. I just need to know you won't try to force anything with us."

He reached a hand out to me, and I took it in mine.

"Friends?" he asked.

"Of course."

His body language suggested he wanted to step closer, but kept himself from doing so.

"So your dad's here for a few days?"

"I guess so. Somehow their thing in Kenya being interrupted is my fault, of course," I said with a sigh as our hand-holding-session ended.

"You going to dinner tonight?"

"Nah. I have plans."

"If you don't want to be around me I understand. I can skip it if you want to go."

"Spending an evening with Helen? Please." I rolled my eyes in dramatic exaggeration. "I just have other plans already."

"With that guy?"

I nodded. "Saul."

"You sure you're safe with him? I mean none of us know him."

"I'm sure. He's a good guy, Ev. I promise."

He sighed and crossed his arms over his chest and looked down at his feet. "Okay. Just..." he trailed off.

"Just what?"

"Just be careful."

"I will." I grabbed his hand again and squeezed gently to reassure him. "Ev?"

"Yeah?"

"Thanks for talking to me."

He smiled.

***

After Everett and I had a heart to heart in the kitchen, we walked back to the living room together. Helen was busy adjusting the hem of her beige jacket and fluffing her floral silk scarf in an attempt to look sophisticated while my father was kissing Justine on the cheek.

"Hattie. We're headed out to check in at our hotel. Hope to see you for dinner," said my father.

I didn't bother to respond, since he obviously didn't care about anything going on in my life that might be important to me.

"Dinner?"

I turned to the chair in the corner, where I saw Saul sitting.

"Saul?"

He stood and walked to me, kissing me on the cheek. I could sense Everett tense beside me.

"When did you get here?" I asked, surprised that he was suddenly in the room with me.

"Just a minute ago. I hope you don't mind, your brother let me in." He extended a hand to Everett, who took it hesitantly. "Everett. Good to see you again."

"Saul."

The entire room felt tense and I was pretty sure I wasn't imagining it.

"Hattie, what's up with dinner plans tonight?" He stepped closer to me and slid my hand into his. I instantly felt calmer.

"Her stepmother and I have just flown in from Kenya, and Hattie here says she's too busy to meet us all for dinner."

"I told you I have plans," I said, trying to keep the anger out of my voice.

"What time?" asked Saul.

"Four-thirty," answered Helen.

I really wished it was acceptable for me to smack her in the face.

"We'll be there," said the man holding my hand.

I looked at him, horrified.

CHAPTER 10 ~ FIRST DATE

Finally settled into the cab of Saul's truck, I frowned at him.

"I don't want to go," I said, being very honest.

He looked at me very seriously, his blue eyes making me want to melt despite my frustrations over family.

"I know you don't, but it makes me look good to get you there." He winked and leaned over, kissing me tenderly. Eventually, he whispered near my ear. "I missed you."

"I missed you too," I said, still sulking.

"Stop pouting? I promise we'll do something fun after dinner."

I sighed. "You don't know how irritating she is."

"Who?"

"Helen." I looked over at him as he pulled away from my house. "My stepmother."

"You can tell me all about it tonight," he said. "If you want."

"What do you want to do until dinner?" I asked.

He glanced at the clock on the truck dash.

"We have an hour. How about a drink? There's a little bar I found that's pretty quiet."

"Sure. Might help me get through dinner."

"Cheer up, sweet thing. I'll make sure you have fun."

He sped up as he hit the main highway, and I felt his warm hand on my knee. We drove in silence, aside from the quiet hum of classical music from the radio. I watched the landscape outside the window as we drove by. Dark clouds were rolling in, as if mocking my mood.

"Penny for your thoughts," said Saul as he turned the radio off.

"It looks like it's gonna rain," I said lazily.

As if the sky heard me, drops began to splatter the windshield.

"You're quite the weather lady," he said, chuckling.

"Sorry I'm in a bad mood."

"The bar's just up ahead. I'll have you feeling better soon enough."

"You're sweet."

"As pie."

The Tracks was a hole-in-the-wall bar and grill tucked behind a small strip mall not far outside of Anacortes. It was situated halfway below ground, underneath a book store. The stairs down were steep, and I gladly held onto Saul's hand as I stepped down just in front of him. Music from the 90's was playing in the background, but thankfully not too loudly. I had hoped for some quiet time.

"Mind if we take a booth in the back?" asked Saul.

"That's fine." I smiled at him sweetly.

He kept hold of my hand and I followed him to a booth with brown vinyl seats. I slid in ahead of him, and he sat beside me. I tucked my purse onto the bench beside me, next to the wall. There weren't many other people near us, just an older couple sitting at the bar and a single man at a small table near the center of the room.

"You and Everett okay?" he asked.

I looked at him and smiled gently. "Yeah. He apologized. I forgave."

"Good. He seems like an okay guy other than being a jerk to my girl."

"We've been friends a long time."

A waitress walked up to our table. She wore a tank top and a short black skirt that showed off her long legs. Her bright red hair was tied up in an intricate bun.

"Welcome to The Tracks," she said. "My name's Carrie. What can I get for you two?"

"I'll have a Mac & Jack's Amber, on tap."

"Great choice," answered the waitress. "And for the lady?"

"Know what you want, babe?"

"I'll have the same."

I had no idea what a Mack & Jacks Amber was, but figured I'd give it a try.

"I'll just need to see some ID, sorry."

"No problem," said Saul. He fished his wallet out of his pocket and handed her his driver's license.

"Ah, cool," said Carrie. "You and I have the same birthday! Down to the year."

"Well happy birthday," said Saul.

"Sweet twenty-four," she said with a smile.

I handed the waitress my own license, and she looked it over before handing it back with a smile.

Carrie left our table and I looked over at Saul.

"When's your birthday?" I asked out of curiosity.

"May first."

"I just missed it?"

"Yup," he said with a smile.

"Can I ask you for a huge favor?" I asked.

"Sure."

"Is it ok if after dinner we just go to your place? Just have a quiet night?"

"Of course. Anything you want."

"Sorry plans got all screwed up."

"I'm not. As long as I get to hang out with you."

He kissed the top of my head and mumbled something about sunshine and honey. The waitress came back over with our two beers and a bowl of ice cream with chocolate syrup and whip cream.

"On the house," she said. "For a belated birthday."

"Thanks, Carrie," said Saul. I liked how he called her by her name. I thought it was pretty classy.

"Anytime. Just let me know if I can get you anything else," she said as she set two napkins and spoons down.

"That was sweet," I said.

Saul held a small spoonful of ice cream smothered in chocolate up for me to taste. I did so, my eyes never leaving his.

"Good?" he asked.

I nodded. "Very. You should try it."

He leaned forward and softly placed his lips on mine, opening my mouth gently. His tongue was warm in my frozen mouth, and he groaned as he tasted both me and the ice cream. The feel of his hand running through my hair as he deepened the kiss made me feel warm inside, and left me near breathless. He ended the kiss as suddenly as he had begun.

"Yup, it's delicious," he said. His voice was deep and husky, and filled with desire.

"You're kinda driving me crazy," I whispered.

"I hope so. I told you I'll make sure you have fun tonight."

"Let's skip dinner," I answered.

"No way."

I sighed.

***

We finished our beers and most of the ice cream before Saul paid and we headed back to his truck. I had offered to pay for my own, but he just rolled his eyes at me.

The drive from the bar to the steak house was short. We arrived a few minutes early, so sat in the truck to talk.

"Promise me we can leave if Helen starts talking about her garden gnome collection?"

Saul laughed. "We'll just show up, eat, and leave. Does she really collect garden gnomes?"

"Uh huh."

"You ready?"

I took a deep breath and looked at him. "I guess so."

"Okay, let's go eat steak."

We both stepped out of the truck, and Saul met me on the passenger side. He offered me his arm like a gentleman, and I wrapped my hand around his elbow. We walked together and it felt safe. It felt right.

He held the restaurant door open for me and I stepped into the dimly lit interior. I hadn't been to Myrtle's in years and it looked just the same as I recalled; cowboy hats and boot spurs on the walls, tall booth backs for privacy, and battery-operated flickering "candles" placed strategically for mood lighting. The walls were wood paneled and the ceiling was made from timbers and smaller logs. In the center of the restaurant hung a chandelier made from an old wagon wheel. It was cheesy overall, but they had good food and the service was well known for being fast and friendly. We walked up to the reception podium and a young clean-cut man with dark skin and light green eyes greeted us.

"Welcome to Myrtle's. Two of you tonight?"

I shook my head. "We're meeting six others."

"Name?" asked the young man.

"Leonardo."

"Ah, yes. We have your table ready, but you're the first here. Would you like to be seated?"

"Please," answered Saul.

"Right this way."

We followed the greeter to a large table in a back room. The table was circular, which I knew meant that no matter where I sat I'd be forced to look at my annoying stepmother. Saul and I walked around to the back of the table and sat beside one another.

"Can I start you with something to drink?" asked the greeter.

"Hattie, what would you like?"

"Lemonade if you have it?"

"We sure do. And you, sir?"

"Coffee, black. And a glass of water, no ice."

"I'll have those right out."

As the man left us, I looked at Saul and smiled.

"That ice cream was good," I said, smirking.

"Best I've ever had," he winked.

"I'm starving," I said.

I looked at my new phone to check the time. Watches had always bothered me, so I was used to relying on my cell.

"Hattie," I heard my father's voice.

Saul stood and extended a hand to my father. I stayed seated as Helen took her jacket off and hung it on the back of her chair.

"Good to see you again, Mr. Leonardo," said Saul.
"Please, just Jim."
"Alright. Jim."

My father and his wife both sat across from us, leaving two open seats between them and us on either side.

"Manda and Everett are right behind us. Joe called and he and Justine are running ten minutes late."

Helen began inspecting her silverware as if it were diseased. A waitress walked up and introduced herself as Ellie, and delivered our beverages. Helen pointed out what was likely an invisible speck of dust on her spoon and asked for a new place setting. She and my fathered both ordered wine and once Ellie left Everett and Miranda joined us. It was a bit awkward when Everett sat beside me, sandwiching me between him and Saul.

"So, Saul and Hattie," said my father with a fake smile. "How did you two meet?"

Saul finished a sip of his coffee and smiled back. "We met over in Fidalgo by the flower shop. Hattie was having a bit of a bad day, so I helped her out and gave her a ride home."

"A ride home?" said Helen, sounding exasperated. "When you didn't know him? That doesn't seem like very bright thinking, Hattie."

"Well, Helen, I guess I had a lot on my mind at the time." I imagined myself throwing my glass of lemonade at her. Saul's hand on my thigh under the table helped calm me.

"It was the day of the explosion," explained Saul. "I couldn't very well leave a pretty lady alone down there amongst the rubble."

"Saul?" asked Miranda. "You were there?"

"Yes, ma'am, I was."

"He actually saved me," I said, locking eyes with him and blocking out the rest of the world for a brief moment.

"So you've known each other what, two days?" asked Everett.

I ignored him. "Saul saved a baby too."

"Oh God, I heard about that on the news. That poor baby died yesterday," blurted out step-bitch.

I looked at Helen and blinked, not quite understanding what she had said.

"What? No, Saul got it out."

I felt Saul tense beside me and heard him sigh.

"Smoke inhalation did it in. The poor thing never stood a chance," continued Helen.

I found Saul's hand with my own and took it, feeling myself tremble. He leaned over and whispered. "I'm sorry, Hattie. I was going to tell you later tonight."

I felt my eyes fill with tears and focused on just breathing.

"Her mother died too, from a head wound. Probably best that they're together now," said Helen.

"You are such a clueless bitch." The words were out of my mouth before I could stop them.

"Pardon me, missy, you best watch that lippy mouth of yours," she hissed at me.

"Ladies, please. Hattie's been through a lot the past couple of days. Let's all try to just calm down," said Miranda.

As usual, my father sat there unspeaking, letting Helen wear the proverbial pants. He used to dote over me and Joe, once upon a time. I stood, intent on going to the restroom to compose myself. Saul kept hold of my hand, standing with me.

"Excuse us," he said.

I walked back through the restaurant until I found the ladies room. I could feel Saul right behind me.

"You gonna be ok?" he asked softly.

"I'll have to be. I just don't want to be here right now."

"Sorry your step is so rotten. I can see what you meant about her."

He wrapped his arms around me and I nestled into his chest, loving the feel of his muscles beneath his tight white t-shirt.

"Take my truck keys, okay? I'll go settle our drink bill and let them know we're leaving. I'll meet you at the truck." He kissed my forehead and gave me a last little squeeze.

"Thanks," I whispered.

He slipped his keys into my hand and I felt instant relief.

CHAPTER 11 ~ AFTERMATH

As I sat in Saul's truck, the engine on and CD playing softly, I closed my eyes and leaned my head back. I was exhausted, likely from the stress of the past hours and days. It was hard to keep the images of the explosion out of my head. The reality of how many people had died began to sink in and knowing that the baby Saul had saved was now gone from the world was nearly too much to bear. I was unable to fathom why a life had been taken so young. I willed my breathing to slow.

I was startled when the truck door finally opened.

"Hey, easy, it's just me," said Saul with a worried look.

I nodded. He stepped into the cab and sat beside me. Just after shutting his door he turned to face me and enveloped my hand in his.

"You father wants me to take you home so he can talk to you."

"Saul, no..."

"Shhh. Just listen. I told him I'd leave it up to you."

"I can't deal with him right now."

I looked him in the eyes.

"I understand, Hattie. I do. You have enough to deal with as it is."

"None of them were there. They don't understand. Please, can I come home with you tonight?"

"Of course you can," he said as he leaned forward and kissed me gently on the lips. His smell was intoxicating. "We'll grab some take-out on the way. Is Chinese okay?"

"Sure," I breathed against his cheek. "Anything's fine as long as I'm with you tonight."

***

We drove for several minutes not talking. It was an unusually comfortable silence. After a while Saul slowed the truck and pulled into a small parking lot. It was a red building with bright yellow trim that looked like at one time it had been a fast food joint, complete with an old drive-up window. The sign out front read *The Peking Duck*.

"Best Chinese in town, I hear," said Saul with a little smile.

I looked at him sideways and he chuckled. "What's funny?"

He kissed my cheek. "Just a bad joke. It's the only Chinese place in town." He winked at me and his smile grew.

"Oh God," I moaned, exaggerating despair. "Don't tell me you're a dork."

"Without a doubt, I am," he laughed again.

"I like your laugh," I said, more seriously.

"And I like you," he returned. "Do you want to wait here or come in with me?" he asked.

"I'll come with."

"Alrighty then. Let's go get 'er done."

"Dork," I said under my breath, teasing him.

"You know it," he whispered back, into my ear. His breath sent shivers up my arms.

We both climbed out of the truck and stretched before going into the restaurant. As we met at the rear of his truck, he took my hand in his. We walked hand-in-hand to the door, which he held open for me.

"You don't have to hold it open," I said.

"I know, but if I didn't I'd feel like a louse."

We walked to the counter together.

"Two for dinner today?" asked a young host.

"We're actually picking up an order for Meyers," said my companion.

I looked at him slyly. "When did you call it in?"

"Oh, back at the steakhouse just before I left."

"Clever man."

"Nah, just a dork," he said, flashing his smile at me again.

The host walked to the kitchen and returned with two plastic sacks. "That'll be $26.12."

Saul pulled out his wallet and counted through some cash.

"Saul, let me pay for half?" I asked.

He stopped leafing through the bills and looked at me for a moment as if he were deep in thought. He shook his head side to side just twice and continued. Pulling out two bills, he handed them to the host.

"Keep the change, man."

"Thank you, and enjoy your meal," said the man.

I brushed a couple of loose hairs behind my ear and took one of the two bags when Saul handed it to me.

Once we were through the doors and back outside, Saul spoke. "Thanks for offering to pay, but not on this date, okay?"

I looked over to him and nodded. "Okay."

"Let's get this home before it gets cold."

I smiled and walked with him to the truck. We set the two sacks between us and started on the road again.

"Smells good," I said. "What did you order?"

"Wonton soup, fried rice, and Mongolian chicken."

"Yum."

"I should have asked if you like it spicy."

"I'm sure I can handle it."

He glanced sideways at me and grinned.

***

The rest of the drive went by quickly. I carried my purse to the door while he took both sacks of Chinese food. The smell in the truck had driven my stomach wild, and it was now growling with hunger. Sitting beside Saul had made me hunger in other ways. I waited patiently as he unlocked the front door, and followed him inside. The house was much brighter than the last time I had been there. Curtains were open and it felt welcoming.

"Do you want to eat in the kitchen or living room?"

"It doesn't matter," I answered. "Either one."

"It's chilly in here. How about I light a quick fire and we can have a picnic in the living room?"

"Sounds great."

"Mind throwing a blanket on the floor and setting the food out?" he asked me.

"Sure."

He closed the front door and walked over to me, standing close. He leaned down and rubbed the tip of his nose against my cheek. My entire body began to relax from the simple gesture. As I began to close my eyes, he slid the plastic bags of food into my hands.

"Let's hurry. I'm starving," he whispered. I wondered if his words held a secret meaning.

Soon the fire was lit and the blanket spread. We sat across from each other with our legs crossed, eating straight from the containers, using chop sticks. I hadn't had much of an appetite since the explosion and it felt good to indulge.

"How is it?" Saul asked me.

"Good," I said after swallowing a bite of Mongolian chicken. "But it's gonna leave behind some serious onion breath."

"I suppose it's a good thing I like onions then," he said with a chuckle.

"I like you, Saul. You're funny."

"I try my best," he said as he set his chopsticks down on a napkin. "And I like you too."

"Can I ask you something?"

"Of course. Anything."

"Was it wrong of me? To leave dinner?"

He leaned back, resting on his arms, and uncrossed his legs. "I think right now, whatever you need to do for yourself is the right thing. Within reason, of course. You've been through a really horrific experience, and it's just gonna take time."

The fire was warming the room finally. I set my own chopsticks down and closed the container of chicken, setting it aside.

"Looks like there's leftovers," I said.

"We can have them tomorrow. I'll go toss 'em in the fridge."

"Want me to do that?" I asked.

"Nah, I need to change my shirt anyway. Dropped Mongolian on it."

He stood and gathered the food containers and left the room. I stood and walked to a wall that housed a bank of bookshelves. Some held books, all hard bound, and others held framed photos and a few odds-n-ends.

The room had begun to grow darker with evening approaching and shadows were creeping into the corners. The firelight was soothing. I turned when I heard Saul returning from the kitchen.

"Hey," I whispered.

"Hey yourself. I brought some wine in if you want some?"

He held out two cobalt blue wine glasses and a bottle of red wine. I wasn't a big wine drinker, but after the surprise appearance of my father and his wife, I nodded my head. He walked to the coffee table, where he poured each glass about half full.

"Nice shirt," I said.

He had come back wearing a button-up in vertical yellow and gray stripes. I turned back to the photos on his shelves. One of them in particular was of an older man and a young boy holding fishing poles. The boy held a fishing string with five trout, all of them on the small side. The older man had an arm around him and both were grinning.

I could sense Saul standing behind me.

"Is that you?" I asked.

"Uh-huh. I was oh…maybe nine years old there? And that was my Pops: my grandpa. He used to take me fishing every summer. Just me and him."

"He loved you," I said absently.

"The feeling was mutual."

"This was his place?"

"Yup. He died last year. My sister and I were probably the only ones who ever went to visit him once he went senile. His own kids put him in a group home, but the staff said no one else ever came to visit except me and Lina. I would have come to live with him here instead of putting him in that home, but my aunt and uncle refused." He sighed heavily. "They trumped me in 'next of kin' order."

"And in the end he willed the place to you?"

"Yeah. He left it all to me and my sister. The house, the land, and what money was left. Oh man, the looks on their faces when the attorney read the will."

"Sounds like you were good to him, Saul."

"I'd give it all back to have him here again. Grandpa Perry was the greatest guy. Kind, gentle, and funny as heck. When my own folks passed away I was only twenty. He was the only one who helped me out. I was an adult according to the rest of the family, so should be able to fend for myself. The truth is I was a mess. My sister was just sixteen, but they had the same opinion there. Pops left her enough money for college, so she headed to the East Coast as soon as she was able to access her part of the trust when she turned twenty this year."

I turned to face him and took the glass of wine that he held out. "Do you think she'll ever come home?" I asked.

He shrugged. "It's hard to say. Our parents dying was hard on us both, but especially her. I fly back to Virginia a couple times a year to check on her."

"Mind if I ask how your parents died?" I took a sip of the wine and found it to be unexpectedly smooth and palatable.

He took my free hand in his and led me to the couch, where we both sat. I situated myself sideways to face him and drew my feet up underneath myself.

"It was an airplane crash. My dad was a pilot. Small aircraft. They were flying up in Alaska for their anniversary and the plane went down. The mayday tapes mentioned engine trouble."

"God, I'm so sorry." I placed a hand on his thigh.

He took a drink of wine and hung his head. "They were good people, like my grandpa. They lived good lives. I'm glad for that."

He set his hand on top of mine and we sat quietly while staring at the fire. The sun was setting in earnest.

"How'd you find out about the baby?" I asked, breaking the silence.

"I went over to the hospital to ask about her. There was a news crew there. I guess I just felt a need to check on the little one."

"I was thinking," I said after taking a drink of the wine. "If you would have gotten to the baby first, instead of me, maybe she would have lived."

"You know who lives and who dies isn't in our control, Hattie."

I looked down at my lap and nodded. "But she was just a tiny baby. What am I in this world? Just some…nobody."

"No, never say that. You're so much more than you think."

I finished my wine in one long drink, the warming sensation it left going down my throat a bit unnerving. Saul held his arms out to signal me closer, and I leaned over so that he could hold me. His arm around me was heavy and warm. I yawned, feeling the wine begin to weave its wicked little grip around me.

"Is it okay if I stay tonight?"

"More than okay. If it were up to me I might just keep you around for a long time."

He moved a bit so that he could easily lean down to kiss me. His lips felt hot on mine and his kiss tasted of sweet wine.

"I'm sorry you had to hear about the baby like you did," he breathed. "But even more than that, I'm sorry you're hurting so much."

Before I could respond his mouth found mine once again and he kissed me with passion. His hands gently slid my sweater down over my shoulders and as our kissing mutually deepened, I shrugged the sweater off. His hands were gentle in discovering my bare skin, as my layered tank tops did little to cover much of me. Not meaning to, I whimpered into him as he moved his mouth to my neck.

"You okay?" he asked, his voice gentle and full of concern.

"Yeah. It just feels good," I said. His mouth began to explore my skin and as he tasted me with his warm tongue, I continued. "Really good."

"Let me make it feel even better?" he groaned.

His hands found their way up my shirts and he reached around to unhook my bra. I leaned forward to make it easier, and quickly he was helping me remove all my layers. He buried his face between my breasts and his hot breath nearly made me melt.

I struggled with the buttons on his shirt until each was freed. I found his waistband and untucked his top, moving my hands up his sides to feel his skin. He was softer than his rugged looks let on and his hard muscles contracted under my touch. The wine was making me feel dizzy and the effect of that mixed with his touch was electric. His mouth found one of my bare breasts and he twisted his tongue lightly around my nipple as he sucked gently. He was being so tender with me and I found myself getting lost in his affections.

"Hattie?" he said quietly as he released my breast to look up at me.

"Hmm?"

"Is it okay if I make love to you?"

I nodded approval and he sat back to take his shirt the rest of the way off. As his button-up fell off, it left him in an undershirt. I leaned forward and eagerly helped lift it above his head. His chest was sculpted and I ran a hand over one of his pecs. I could feel his eyes on me as I slowly explored the curves of his chest. His body was mesmerizing. I leaned forward and kissed him softly next to his left nipple. I heard him groan lightly, and took it as a cue to continue. I moved my mouth, trailing along until I felt his nipple beneath my lips. I gently drew his small nub into my mouth, tasting the saltiness of his skin. I really hadn't a clue as to what I was doing, but his reaction told me that I was doing it well. As I got more involved, he winced.

"Not too hard, babe." He sounded breathless.

I stopped and looked at him. I could feel my heart pounding with longing. Saul readjusted on the couch, eventually standing. He held an arm out for me, and I took his hand as I stood.

"Bedroom or here?" he asked.

"I'm not sure I can make it to the bedroom," I huffed.

I reached forward and began to undo his belt. His jeans were tight from his erection and he was obviously uncomfortable.

"Here, I'll get it," he said, his voice even deeper than usual.

As he worked the buckle of his belt until it was undone, I began undoing my own jeans button.

"No, let me? Please?" he asked, interrupting me. "It kind of turns me on," he explained.

I stopped and watched him slide his pants down. He was wearing boxers in gray and burgundy plaid, and they did little to hide his hardness. He moved forward and began working at the front of my pants.

"I've never seen anything as beautiful as you," he whispered.

He slid my pants down with obvious expertise, and stepped closer. Wrapping his arms around my nearly nude body, he kissed me hard. I reached my arms up and wrapped them around his shoulders, pulling myself against him in an effort to get even closer, if that was possible. His thumbs hooked into the sides of my panties and he tugged them down. Eventually they fell to my feet and I kicked them off. Saul lifted me off the floor and I wrapped my legs around him as he backed up closer to the fireplace. His cock was pressing into me, eagerly searching. He carefully lay me down on the blankets where we had eaten dinner. I reached up and again traced the lines of his chest with my index finger, slowly trailing down to his abs. I felt his body shiver under my touch. As my fingers got to his boxers, I used both hands to tug them down to his hips. He pulled them down the rest of the way and continued to explore my body with his mouth, his hands, and his manhood. I could feel my own dampness between my legs and was more than ready for him to enter me.

"God I need you," I moaned.

"Yeah?"

"Yeah."

I felt his hand slide between my legs and he groaned loudly.

"Fuck, you're so wet…"

He dipped one of his fingers inside of me, and using my own wetness he began pleasuring me by tracing tiny circles on my clit with his fingertip.

"You like that, don't you?" his voice was near-growling.

"Yeah," I managed to breathe out. "I really like that."

His finger suddenly slid back inside of me, going deeper than before, and I felt him stroke my inner walls playfully. He continued, this time teasing my nub with his thumb while his finger searched deep within me. The combination made me arch my back and lift my hips in desire. I could feel his hard cock stroking my leg and he began breathing heavily.

"I know I need to grab a condom, Hattie, but can I just feel you for a second?"

I wasn't really sure how to answer. At the time all I knew was that I wanted him inside of me so badly that I was ready to cry out, begging for it.

"Just for a second? I promise," he whimped.

He nuzzled his face against my chest and moved his hands to my arms, which I lifted over my head as he rearranged himself to lay on top of me. His cock was hard against me and I felt the tip slide against my dampness. As it touched my clit, I groaned. I let my legs fall open, inviting him to feel me any way that he needed to. His touch was light in exploring me as he slid his erection up and back down my folds, occasionally dipping the head in just half an inch or so.

His whole body began tensing and I couldn't make myself stay quiet. My whimpering soon turned to gasping as he began to enter me just a tiny bit more. Every shred of my being wanted to become one with him in that moment.

"I have to stop, baby," he said in little gasps.

"No," I whispered. "No," I pleaded.

"It'll just take me a minute, I promise."

"Don't go?" I begged, letting my knees fall to the sides even more. I reached down and touched myself, desperate for my fingers to be him inside of me. "Please, Saul?"

He leaned down and kissed my mouth. I could tell he was torn between what he knew was right and what he knew we both wanted. I moved my hands to his back and kneaded at his flesh while his cock again found its target. He slid the tip inside of me again and hesitated.

"Just for a minute," he whispered while looking me in the eyes tenderly.

I barely nodded, but knew it was just enough for him to take my cue. He moved his cock carefully into me, this time half-way. I moaned with the pleasure, causing him to stop and his entire body felt tense on top of me. He looked at me again and I nodded as I stared back into his eyes.

"Just for a minute," he groaned as he buried himself into me slowly and deeply. It felt so good that my body begged for more by grinding against him. His eyes closed as he matched my rhythm, allowing him to go even deeper when our bodies met. Eventually he opened his eyes and watched me while we danced together. As he began thrusting faster, he had a pained look on his face.

"We have to stop, babe. Seriously."

"Just for another minute?"

"I can't. I can't hold it that long."

He slowed, to my dismay. I must have looked pathetically sad, because he leaned down and kissed my forehead, still lingering inside of me. He very slowly began pumping into me again, looking at my face the entire time as if watching for me to say "stop." I never did. He continued on, slowly and almost hesitantly, for a long time. Eventually he sped his thrusting up, breaking his eye-lock with me. We both allowed ourselves to get lost in the pleasure and eventually fell apart in each other's arms.

Both of us exhausted, we lay on the floor side-by-side, allowing the heat of the fire and the heat of each other to warm us. We didn't talk, but rather fell asleep with our bodies entwined with each other.

CHAPTER 12 ~ A VISITOR

We slept on the living room floor for hours. It was a knock on the front door that roused me from a restless sleep. I woke wrapped in Saul's arms, wondering if I had dreamt the knocking. The fire was dying, the room lit only by glowing red and orange embers. I snuggled up closer to Saul and closed my eyes again. The knock came again. This time louder.

"Saul?" I whispered. He was sleeping deeply and didn't respond, so I gently shook his shoulder. "Saul?"

"Hmm?" He sounded exhausted.

"Someone's knocking on your door."

His eyes fluttered open at my words.

"What time is it?" he mumbled.

"I'm not sure. I left my phone on the coffee table."

"Okay, hang on. I'll see who it is and get rid of them."

Whoever it was knocked again, this time calling out Saul's name.

"Saul! Open up, it's me, Carolina!"

I heard him struggle to slip into his jeans, grumbling as he collided against the coffee table.

"Hattie, it's my sister. Mind slipping some clothes on?" he asked me quietly.

"Did you know she's in town?"

"No…"

I stood and grabbed what looked like my shirts sitting in a heap on the floor. "I'll get dressed in the bathroom," I said quietly.

"Lina, hang on!" he called out. "I'll be there in a sec!"

Zipping his fly, he leaned down and kissed me on the cheek. I gathered my jeans and panties and stumbled in the dark to where I recalled the bathroom being. Half way there, he turned the kitchen light on. I snuck into the bathroom and hurried to do girly business and dress. My sweater, one tank, and bra were missing, so I settled for my jeans and a single tank top. I could hear Saul and Carolina greeting each other. She was busy apologizing for arriving in the middle of the night and he was telling her that she's welcome at any time - 24/7. I quickly borrowed a dab of Saul's toothpaste and used my finger to scrub my teeth, hoping to rid myself of a horrible Chinese food and wine aftertaste. I ran my fingers through my hair and took a deep breath.

Never being the best at meeting new people, I forced myself to calm down and leave the safety of the bathroom. As I walked down the hall I could hear the clinking of dishes coming from the kitchen. Saul's sister was busy asking him why he hadn't returned her e-mails.

"Hold on, sis," he said, sounding exasperated. "You know I hate e-mail. Why didn't you call?"

As they grew within my sight, I slowed down, crossed my arms over my chest to hide my lack of a bra, and cleared my throat.

"Oh, hey, Lina. This is Hattie."

He was standing there in bare feet and a bare chest, wearing only his jeans.

"Oh, God. I didn't know you had company," she said, obviously embarrassed to have interrupted our night.

I smiled at her. My first impression was that she was a sweet girl, likely taking after her older brother.

"It's okay," I mumbled. "Really."

Saul held an arm out, indicating I should step beside him. As I did so, Carolina stood and walked toward us. She held a hand out and I took hers in mine.

"Good to meet you," she said.

"Hattie, I'm just making tea. Do you want some?" Saul asked me.

"Yeah, sure."

"Lina flew in because she hadn't heard from me since the explosion. I guess I didn't check my e-mail and she didn't check her texts."

"Oops," I said. "You must have been really worried about him."

"Yeah, that's an understatement," said the girl with a soft smile.

She looked a bit like her brother with the same coloring but finer features, as well as being a head shorter.

"How long are you in town for?" Saul asked.

"Just a couple days. I have to get back to work, stuff like that."

"How'd you get from the airport to here?"

He was busy pouring hot water into three mugs.

"I rented a car. No biggie."

"Your bags out front?" he asked.

Lina nodded.

"I'll grab them."

"Saul, I can stay at a hotel. It's not a big deal."

"Nonsense," he said. "You know you're always welcome here."

"Still have a couch?" she asked.

"I do. I'd let you crash in my bed and take the couch but Hattie's staying here tonight."

"I can head home if you want, Saul," I offered.

"No...don't do that!" said Lina. "I'm totally fine on the couch."

Of course I felt bad, and the situation was a bit awkward.

"What time is it anyway?" asked Saul, yawning.

Lina looked at her watch and followed suit with yawning. "Almost two o'clock."

"Hattie, do you mind finishing the tea while I grab Lina's bags?"

"Sure. No problem."

Of course it meant uncrossing my arms, but I took his place in front of the steaming mugs and added tea bags to each as he walked outside to gather luggage.

"So where did you guys meet?" his sister asked me.

I looked up and tucked a few stray hairs behind my left ear. "The explosion," I said. "He saved me."

"Seriously? Wow...that's so like him."

"Yeah I was pretty lucky. I guess we both were. You know, to make it out of there."

"The list of deceased didn't have his name on it, but I was so worried since he didn't answer my e-mails or calls."

"He never mentioned you calling," I said quietly in his defense.

"He probably changed his number again. He's had to do that a couple of times with the big family feud going on."

"You girls behaving?" came Saul's voice from the front door. He had left it open and the cold of the night was creeping in. I could feel goose bumps on my bare arms.

"Of course not, Saul," said Lina, obviously joking.

"Just the three bags Lina?"

"Yup. Thanks for hauling them in."

"Anytime. I know you're a wimp and all."

She swatted at him and rolled her eyes.

"Hattie you look half frozen. I'll add some logs to the stove."

"Let's take the tea in there," suggested Lina. "It's always been the warmest room. I had forgotten how cold it is here this time of year."

"Days have been pretty warm here," I added. "Nights are still chilly."

Lina carried her mug as well as Saul's and I took my own. We followed him into the living room, where I scurried around picking up our remaining clothes from the floor. I knew I was blushing, but Carolina was tactful enough to not say anything. Saul made quick work of stoking the fire and adding a piece of wood, and picked up the blankets we had slept on without explaining. Lina settled into the only easy chair in the room and slumped into it, looking exhausted. I did nearly the same, settling in on one end of the couch. Saul joined me, sitting close and wrapping an arm around my shoulders.

"So Saul it sounds like you're a big time hero now, huh?" said his sister.

"I guess so," he said, looking at me with a softness in his eyes. That look actually made my stomach do a flip-flop.

"So you guys didn't know each other beforehand?"

"Nope," was all he said, eventually breaking his gaze upon me and looking over at her.

I sipped at my tea, which was warming and soothing.

"I'm so tired," yawned Carolina. "That flight sucked."

"Yeah we should all hit the hay. I'll treat to breakfast at Moe's tomorrow."

A large smile spread across Lina's face, making her look even more like Saul.

"I love Moe's," she said with the faintest of giggles.

"I know you do. I'll grab some blankets and a pillow from the linen closet."

"Thanks, Saul."

Lina looked ready to collapse. I stood to make room for her on the sofa. Gathering the three mugs to return them to the kitchen, Lina looked up at me and smiled. I could tell we'd easily become friends if given a chance. She didn't seem stuck on herself like other girls our age. I liked that.

"Glad I could meet you, Hattie," she said, followed by another yawn.

"Me too. We'll talk more tomorrow, ok?"

She nodded as Saul returned with his arms full of bedding.

"Night, Carolina. Sleep well," I said as I left the two of them alone and walked toward Saul's bedroom.

"I'll be right there, Hattie," called Saul softly as I walked away.

"Okay."

Once in his bedroom, I turned on the lamp on the dresser and gently shut the door. He had made his bed since we had slept there the night before and it looked inviting. I slipped my jeans off, folded them, and set them in an empty chair in the corner. I took notice that he had plugged my cell phone into a charger cord on the nightstand and smiled. I walked to the large area rug that covered most of the floor, hoping to give my bare feet a break from the cold wood beneath them. I could hear Lina and Saul's muffled voices from the other room and figured they might need some time alone to discuss secret sibling stuff, so pulled the covers back and climbed into the bed. The sheets smelled of fresh laundry soap and fabric softener. I slid under the covers and nestled in, hoping my legs would soon warm.

I was just beginning to fall asleep when I heard the door open. I looked up and saw Saul. He looked as tired as I felt.

"Got her all settled in," he said.

"You sure you don't want me to go home?" I asked.

"No chance. It's freezing in here. Who would keep me warm?"

I watched as he slipped his jeans off, leaving just his boxers.

"Mind if I sleep in here?" he asked.

His question made me chuckle. "It's your bed; of course you can sleep in here."

As he turned off the lamp, the room was bathed in darkness. I scooted over to make room for him, glad to have him near me again. I had begun to notice that I felt calmer just by his being near. I could sense him lean down and soon he was kissing me passionately.

"Thanks for staying," he whispered as he backed away.

I cuddled into the crook of his arm, resting my head on his chest.

"Your sister seems really nice."

"Yeah, she's pretty sweet. Always has been."

He ran a toe up my leg, causing me to flinch.

"Your feet are cold," I said quietly.

"Hattie. We need to talk."

His words made my stomach drop.

"Did I do something wrong?"

"No…no. Nothing like that. It's what we did, together. We can't do that again."

"Do what?" I asked, slightly confused.

"Unprotected sex."

"Oh." I could feel my face turn several shades of red in the dark. "Sorry."

"Don't get me wrong, I loved every second of it. I can't even begin to tell you how good you felt…but I don't want to risk anything. I mean, I assume you're not on birth control?"

"This is so embarrassing," I said, burying my face into his chest.

"No, babe…nothing to be embarrassed about. You're gorgeous and what we're doing is fine, really. Never be embarrassed talking to me about it, ok?"

I nodded into his chest.

He continued, now stroking my hair gently. "I just wouldn't want us to get into a situation we're not ready for when we've only known each other for what has it been? Three days?"

"I've never used birth control," I said as I unburied my head from him.

"Do you have a doctor? I mean for women stuff?"

122

"Just my family doctor. She's mentioned pills or shots before, but I've never needed anything. Her office was downtown, though, by the courthouse."

He sighed and kissed my forehead. "Don't get me wrong, I'm happy to keep using condoms. We just can't get carried away like that again."

"It was fun though, wasn't it?"

"Yes, Hattie, you naughty girl."

He ran a hand over my bare thigh, causing me to shiver.

"Okay, so here's the embarrassing part," he sighed. "When's your period due?"

"Ewww," I said.

He chuckled. "It's a serious question."

"Just in a few days," I admitted.

"Good. That means it's not likely you'd get pregnant from tonight."

"That'd suck," I admitted.

"Yeah, right now it would."

"Right now?"

"Well, I kinda like you. Maybe someday?"

I ran a hand down over his crotch, trying to lighten the mood. I was a bit surprised to find him hard again already. I stroked him gently yet firmly, massaging, knowing full well what kind of reaction I would get.

"That's not fair," he said as his breathing deepened.

Being daring, I slipped my hand beneath the waistband of his boxers until I felt the soft hair that surrounded his cock.

"Fuck, Hattie," he gasped.

"Hmm?" I grunted as I began kissing his bare chest, trailing my lips softly down toward his belly button.

Between the two of us, we managed to pull his boxers off.

"You feel so good," he moaned quietly, obviously trying to stay quiet enough that his sister wouldn't hear from the next room.

I climbed on top of him and looked down. My eyes had adjusted to the dark and the little bit of moonlight that streamed in through the window allowed me to see the longing on his face. I sat upright, grinding against his erection as I did so. The sensation was different, since I still had my panties on. I found it exciting, and from his reaction he did too. I pulled my tank top up over my head, slowly revealing my breasts to him. He struggled beneath me, almost as if trying to gain control over the situation. I felt his fingertips caress my breasts, slowly tracing around my nipples. His touch sent shivers up my spine.

"Saul?" I whispered, barely audibly.

"Hmm?"

"Do you have any condoms in here?"

"Oh my God I want to fuck you again," he groaned.

His body tensed and I heard him fumbling in the drawer of the night stand beside us. Soon I heard him opening the foil package of a condom. I pressed down on his cock again, showing him just how badly I wanted him inside of me. Without warning he rolled out from under me, flipping me onto my back. I watched in the pale light of the moon as he unrolled the condom onto his erection. His face looked almost pained from the extra wait. In the next moments he pulled my panties off, almost roughly.

"Do you want it rough or sweet and slow?" he almost growled against my neck.

I wasn't really sure what he meant, so took a chance. "Rough?"

He began sucking on my neck, and I began getting lost in the passion I felt from his touch. I felt him lift me slightly, readjusting me so that I was lying on my back across the bed. He stood and pulled on my thighs, scooting me toward the edge of the bed.

"Okay, but promise you'll tell me if it's too much?"

I felt just the tiniest bit of apprehension as he said that.

"Promise, Hattie?"

I nodded. "I promise."

He spread my legs, scooting me again until my hips were just off of the edge of the bed. He held my legs wide, and guided his cock to my entry. He slid it in, making sure I was ready, and his first full thrust landed deep. He repeated the motion, filling me with more of his manhood than he had before. I gripped at the sheet beneath me, my breath nearly taken away. After the fourth thrust, he slowed.

"Is that okay?" he grunted.

I wasn't sure I could actually speak, so answered by lifting my hips slightly, encouraging him to continue.

"Oh God," he moaned as he began thrusting again. This time it was just as deep, but so much faster. He grunted, almost sounding animalistic.

The initial shock of the way he was fucking me began to ebb and I found myself opening my legs farther, hoping he'd be able to go even deeper. Eventually he leaned forward, finding my wrists above my head, and held my arms down. He continued to deliver thrust after thrust, this time the sensation changed from his angle.

I tried my best to be quiet, but as I shattered into a million pieces of pleasure I called out just a bit too loud. Saul found his release as mine was ending.

CHAPTER 13 ~ MISSING

When we woke the next morning, Lina was missing from the couch. Saul found a note on the kitchen counter.

Went for a morning walk. Be back by 9:30! – Carolina

9:30 came and went. Saul and I had both showered and dressed, although my clothes were stale from the day before.

"Should we go look for her?" I asked Saul as we sat in the kitchen drinking coffee.

He glanced at the clock on the microwave. "It's 10:30. Let's give her another fifteen?"

"Is her phone going straight to voice mail?"

"Yeah. Either it's dead or off, I figure."

"You're worried," I said, deciding to not pussyfoot around the subject.

He sighed heavily. "Yeah."

"Is there anyone we should call?"

He sucked in the left side of his cheek and slowly shook his head side to side. "We have family in the area, but honestly they wouldn't give a rat's ass about Lina or me."

"We should head out and look."

He reached a hand across the small table and placed it over my own. I took that as a 'yes.'

"Leave your cell here? I'll leave a note to call me if she gets back."

"Sure," I said. "I'll go grab it."

It didn't take me long to retrieve my phone from the bedroom, and when I got back to the kitchen Saul was writing his sister a note.

"It's almost 10:45," I said. "Let's get going?"

He nodded. "You sure you want to come with?"

"I insist."

I slipped my sweater on and we left the house, leaving the door unlocked. The rental car was gone, so Lina could have been anywhere.

***

Saul's truck was cold, but the sun was shining and the day held promise of being warm. He wasn't very talkative and seemed tense. Even though we had only known each other for a handful of days, I could tell that he was worried sick about his sister.

"Is there anywhere you can think of that she might go?" I asked, thinking it prudent.

"She used to walk the beach a lot. There's also a park not far that she's fond of. Tide's high, so we'll check the park first."

"You have your cell phone, right?"

He had both hands gripping the steering wheel, so let go with one to feel his chest pocket. "Yeah."

"Want me to hold it?"

"Yeah."

He didn't make a move to hand it to me, so I scooted closer and fished it out of his pocket. I flipped it open to make sure the volume was turned up, and then held it in my hand as we drove. After about five minutes he pulled off onto a small roadway marked with a sign to Mt. Erie Park.

"She used to hike up to the summit," he said. "I'd go with on my days off. We'd sit up there and just watch the view for hours."

He drove the truck down the curving road that led to the trailhead.

"Saul?"

"Yeah?"

"I'm wearing sandals. I don't think I can hike it."

He parked the truck and looked over at me. "I'll take you up there sometime. If you want."

I looked at him and nodded. "Yeah. I'd like that."

I looked out the passenger window and saw a lone figure sitting on top of a picnic table.

"Saul? Is that her?"

Whoever it was had their head hung.

"I think it might be. Come with me?"

He unfastened his seatbelt and opened his door. I did the same, and followed as he speed-walked across a grassy field toward the picnic table.

"Lina?" he called out.

The figure turned at the sound. We were close enough now to identify her. Her eyes were red and swollen from crying.

"Carolina! What's wrong?" Saul asked as he rushed to her side. "Fuck, I was so worried!"

I stood back as he wrapped his arms around her. She didn't answer, but clung to him and began sobbing.

"Shhhh, Lina...what's wrong?" he soothed. "Shhhh."

I stood back a few feet, not wanting to interfere in whatever was going on.

His sister continued to cling to him, sobbing, as a small child might.

"Talk to me, Lina," he urged. "What's happened?"

"He's dead, Saul," she sobbed.

"Who? Lina, you're scaring me."

"Benny. The little boy I took care of."

Saul held Lina out from him so that he could look her in the face.

"The little guy you nanny for? What do you mean he's dead?"

She sniffled, using her sleeve to wipe tears from her eyes. "It was my day off. I never should have left."

"What happened to him?"

I took a couple of steps closer, hoping to help in some way.

"Someone broke into their house." Carolina looked up into Saul's face. "They killed him, Saul. There was blood everywhere."

"Carolina. Who killed him? You need to take a deep breath and explain, baby girl."

I could see her shaking, head to toe.

"I-I-I'm not sure," she stammered. "I think his dad might have been a drug dealer. He always paid me in cash and Benny's mom made a few comments here and there. I always figured I should just mind my own business. When I got back the whole house was dark. Amy and Don always kept lights on and someone was almost always awake. I found them both in the living room, just lying there in blood." She took a shuddering breath. "There was so much blood, Saul. Benny was on the stairs. His legs were underneath him and oh God..." she broke off.

Saul held her head against his chest and smoothed her hair which fell down her back in a sheet of brown.

"I can't go back there," she moaned. "I can't go back to that house."

"When did this happen?" I asked, feeling like I was intruding in a very private family moment. I had stepped close enough to rest a hand on her shoulder.

The girl looked up at me, her face a mess of tears and makeup.

"Just a few days ago. I wasn't sure where else to go."

"What did the police say?" asked Saul. "Do they have any leads?"

She shook her head side to side. "Not that they told me. They know I'm here. They said I'll probably have to go back soon though."

"Ok. If that happens I'll go with you," he offered. "Right now let's get you back home. I'll make breakfast there."

"Saul, take her with you. I'll drive the rental car back," I offered.

He simply nodded at me, his expression full of both sadness for his sister and thanks for my offer.

Lina's rental car was parked in another lot, so Saul drove me to it. Lina stayed in the cab of the truck with him while I got myself situated in her rental car. The engine started without any issues and I backed out of the parking spot. Saul was waiting for me so I could follow them home.

***

By the time we got back to his little house, Lina had managed to compose herself somewhat and was no longer crying. Her face, though, had tell-tale signs that she had been in rough emotional shape.

"Lina, I'll help Saul make some breakfast. Why don't you go take a hot bath?" I suggested.

"Yeah I'm sure I could use one," she admitted.

"You want omelets or pancakes, Sis?" he sked. His voice sounded a bit strained.

"Maybe just scrambled eggs? And coffee?"

"You got it."

Lina excused herself and left for the bathroom.

"Saul? Is she okay?"

He took a deep breath and put his hands on his hips. "I'm not sure."

"How old was the little boy?"

"Maybe five or six? She's been his nanny for a couple months now."

"Crap. I'm really sorry."

He walked to me and wrapped his arms around me. "I've never seen her this upset before."

"She's going to need you. I should probably head home after breakfast; give you guys some time alone."

"You don't have to do that, Hattie Cakes."

I chuckled at the ridiculous pet name he had just made up.

"She'll need your bedroom. I'd say come stay with me, but she needs you here."

He kissed my forehead. "I can take you home, but I can also pick you back up later if you want. Lina won't mind you being here."

"Let's just see how it goes today, okay?"

He responded by kissing my lips sweetly. "Okay."

I got to work on making scrambled eggs while Saul started a fresh pot of coffee. I worked quietly whisking the eggs and a splash of milk together. We held off on cooking them until Lina was done, so while we waited for her I set the table and Saul fished jam and butter from the fridge. He popped bread into his two-slice toaster and I poured two cups of coffee. We sat in the living room until Lina emerged.

"Feeling better?" I asked just before sipping at my coffee.

"A little, thanks."

"Breakfast will only take a few minutes to cook," I said. Why don't you two sit back while I finish up in the kitchen?" I suggested.

"I'll help," she insisted.

"Me too," said Saul with a wink.

We all walked to the kitchen together. I poured Lina a cup of coffee and she took it to the counter, where she added milk and sugar. She hoisted herself up next to the stove top and sat, hot coffee in hand.

"Just kick back, Sis," Saul said teasingly.

"I'm really sorry to dump this on you guys," she mumbled into the steam coming from her mug. "I know you've had your own crap going on."

"I'm really sorry about Benny," I said as I poured the egg mixture into a hot pan on the stove.

"Thanks. He was the greatest kid. Smart, and funny, you know? I just can't get the images of him and his folks out of my mind." She hung her head and looked down at her feet. "I really loved him."

My phone chirped, sounding like a bird in the spring. I was a bit surprised since as far as I knew Saul was the only one with the number. Saul was the closest to it, so peeked at the screen.

"Hattie, it's your brother."

"Joe? How'd he get my number?"

I took the phone from him and slid the bar on the screen to the right, unlocking it. "Hello?"

"Hey Hat, it's Joe. Just making sure you're okay?"

"Yeah I'm fine. Just about to eat breakfast. How'd you get my number?"

"Uh, your boyfriend gave it to me last night."

I glanced at Saul, mean mugging him just slightly. He shrugged at me and winked for good measure. He tossed a pinch of shredded cheese into his mouth and I stuck my tongue out at him playfully. I noticed Lina roll her eyes at us.

"Uh, so what's up?" I asked Joe.

"We're having a barbecue over here tonight. Dad wants you to come."

"Oh God, Joe...I can't take anymore of Helen. Seriously."

"I guess she has some appointment later, so she won't be here. I promise," he said.

"What time?"

"Oh, like four o'clock. I'm gonna throw some t-bones and bratwurst on the barbie. Justine's making her famous baked beans."

I grunted in frustration. I really didn't feel like seeing my father.

"C'mon, Hat. Miranda and Everett will be there. A few other friends. Bring your boy toy."

I felt my face flush. As comfortable as I was with Saul, we had known each other for such a short time that the terms "boyfriend" and "boy toy" made my stomach form a bit of a knot.

"I'll talk to him and let you know in an hour, okay?"

"Sure. Oh and if you come bring some chips?"

"Oh, Joe, I interrupted his thought."

"Huh?"

"Saul's sister is in town."

"Well bring her with, duh."

"I'll call you later. Bye."

I hung up and looked over at Saul, who was dishing the eggs onto the plates.

"What's up, buttercup?" he asked me.

"Joe and Justine are barbecuing tonight. They want us to come."

"Okay," was all he said.

"My dad will be there."

"Okay."

"You guys should go," said Carolina.

"No...Joe said 'well bring her with, duh,'" I said, trying to imitate my brother. "You're more than welcome to come with, Lina. Seriously. I mean if you feel up to it."

"It might be good for you," said Saul as he took the empty frying pan and set it in the sink.

"I dunno," said Lina as she hopped down from the counter.

I heard the toast pop up, so went over to spread butter and strawberry jam on top. I piled it onto a plate and carried it to the table.

"Why don't you want to go?" asked Lina. "If you don't mind me asking?"

Saul shoveled a huge bite of eggs into his mouth and spoke with his mouth full. "You two girls talk about that. I'm eating."

"Rude," said Lina, chuckling. "Close the trap when there's grub in there."

"You sound like Mom," he said with a grin once he had swallowed.

"My dad showed up in town last night. I don't get along with his wife." I took a bite of toast.

"She's a bitch?" asked Lina.

I swallowed. "That's putting it mildly."

"What about your mom? Is she around?"

Saul glared at her in warning.

"It's ok, Saul. Seriously. My mom died when we were born."

"We?"

"Hattie has a twin brother," explained Saul.

"Joe," I added. "Anyway my dad and his wife live on the East Coast. Joe and I live in the house our mom willed to us. It's a sore spot with Helen." I took a sip of coffee. "AKA the megabitch."

"Joe got married two days ago," said Saul.

'Oh, cool. Was it a big wedding?"

I shook my head no. "It was scheduled for the day of the explosion. It would have been small anyway but they went to the Justice of the Peace the next day. Oh! Saul, I forgot to tell you. Justine's having a baby."

He was sipping his coffee and sputtered into the cup, ending with a laugh.

"What's funny?" whispered Lina.

"Is it his?" asked Saul.

I kicked him playfully under the table, causing him to grin. I liked this fun side of him.

"I think it's her neighbors," I said to lighten the overall mood of the morning.

"Well, we should go then," said Saul with a hearty laugh. "You know, congratulate her and the neighbor."

"Dork," I mumbled as I crammed a bite of toast into my mouth.

I felt his hand on my leg. I smiled slyly at him.

"Lina? You'll come?" I asked.

She shrugged. "Sure. But the food better be good."

"Rude," said Saul, teasing her.

She smiled, obviously enjoying the teasing.

"I should get home and help them get ready."

"I'll drive you," offered Saul. "Lina, will you be ok here alone for about an hour or so?"

"Uh...yeah," she said with a roll of her eyes. "What do I look like, a four year old?"

"Nah, I'd say at least ten."

Saul stood and walked to the counter, where he fished his truck keys out of a little wicker basket.

"I'll clear the table and do the dishes," said Lina.

"Thanks, Sis. Hattie Cakes, you ready?"

I sighed. "Yeah. I guess."

"Boy, you look excited," said Lina with a giggle.

I gathered my phone and purse and left the little house with Saul. Oddly, I was just slightly excited about the dreaded barbecue.

CHAPTER 14 ~ PARTY LIGHTS

Saul dropped me off in front of my house, and I kissed him briefly and sweetly on the cheek before opening my door.

"Don't be too long?" I asked, making a pouty face.

"I'll be back with Lina in a couple hours or so. I promise."

"Oh, crap. I forgot. Can you guys pick up some beer and chips?"

"Sure. Any particular kind?"

"Nah. Whatever you want. Maybe Doritos?"

"You got it. See you soon, sweet thing."

I smiled as I slid from the cab of the truck and shut the door. I watched him drive away, took a deep breath, and made my up the walkway to the front door. I only saw Justine's car in the driveway, so was hopeful that my father wasn't there quite yet. I knew I'd have to face him sooner or later, but just wasn't ready. Not today.

The front door was unlocked, a bad habit of Joe's. I let myself in and felt my mood lighten when I saw balloons set around the living room, in blue and pink.

"Justine? Joe? I'm home," I called out.

"We're out back," I heard Justine call back.

I walked to the kitchen and walked through the still-opened sliding door that led to our small cedar deck. Joe had built it himself just the year prior, and I had helped him lay paving stones down below to extend the entertaining area. It had been a fun project, and we were both proud of the results. In one corner of the deck was the charcoal barbecue that Joe insisted upon using. He said the flavor of meat was always better than when cooking with gas. In another corner was a large steel wash basin that had reportedly belonged to our great-grandma Katie. Joe had filled it with ice and cans of beer and soda.

"Looking good out here," I said with a smile. "New patio table?"

"It was a gift from your dad," said Justine, who was glowing. "For our wedding."

"Awesome. I'm surprised Helen approved."

"C'mon, Hat. Be nice."

"Sorry," I grumbled. "Hey, I need to go shower and change."

"Where's the boy toy?" asked Joe, who obviously enjoyed teasing me.

I pouted. "Stop calling him that. He'll be here in a couple hours."

"Sorry."

"Hey, I saw the balloons. Are you announcing the baby tonight?"

"We sure are. Do you want to help set them up when you're done getting ready?" asked Justine. "We're going to tie them to the patio rail."

"Awesome. I'll be down in about half an hour and start bringing them out."

***

I hurried in the shower and dried my hair until it was straight. I decided to wear it down, keeping it simple. I figured since it was a special occasion I might as well put on some light makeup to make my eyes stand out. After a quick spray of my favorite perfume, I made sure my towel was wrapped around myself tightly and walked across the hall to my bedroom. I picked out a pale blue sundress with cream-colored tropical flowers. The dress fell to just above my knees. I left my arm uncovered where my skin was still marred from the explosion several days earlier. It was healing and the bandage was a bother. I settled on a pair of cream-colored flip-flops and hurried back downstairs.

The living room was still filled with balloons and I could hear Justine laughing from the backyard. I grabbed a handful of the balloons and walked them to the patio, where Joe and I began tying them to the rail. My mood instantly dropped when I heard my father's voice coming from inside the house. I had expected at least another hour before anyone arrived.

"Hey there, Hattie Girl!" boomed my father's voice. He sounded unusually chipper.

"Jim, come help me with this!" It was the grating voice of Helen.

"Be right there, darling!"

"I thought Helen had something else to do," I said with a sigh.

"Well, she decided she should be here. Cut her some slack, please? She really is trying, Hattie," said my father.

"She doesn't try to do anything nice."

"Come on, this is Joe's day. Just try for one day. I need to go help Helen bring in the meat for the barbecue."

I watched as my father walked back into the house and out of habit rolled my eyes at his back. I tied the last three balloons onto the rail before glancing down to the patio, where Joe and Justine were cleaning the grill together.

"Hey guys, balloons are all out. I need to run back upstairs but will be down soon. Dad's here; says he brought meat. And Helen."

"Thanks Hattie," called back Justine.

As much as I despised my stepmother I knew that my dad was right. The day belonged to my brother, his new wife, and their new baby. I could go back to hating Helen tomorrow. On my way back through the house, my father and his wife were busy making their way to the kitchen. His arms were full of steaks and sausages while hers were empty. She was wearing a cranberry colored business suit, high heels, and a string of gaudy fake pearls. She had obviously just had her hair done. It had been bleached platinum blonde. She wore it in a spiky short hair do and it was rather obvious that she thought she looked like a high-class piece of fancy ass. I did my best to not outright laugh.

"Hattie. Nice to see you," she said to me in an obviously forced sing-song voice.

I could hear a couple of Joe's friends coming into the kitchen behind us. They were busy greeting my father and helping him with his arms full of meat.

"Helen. Don't you just look…lovely," I said while still trying to stifle laughter.

The woman looked at me for a long moment without saying anything. It was rare to see her speechless.

"Are you going to change soon?" asked Helen.

I looked down at my own dress and smoothed the sides of the skirt with my palms. Looking back up at her I simply smiled and said "no."

"Well, it's a bit revealing, don't you think?"

"Nope," was all I said in reply.

The dress showed just a touch of my cleavage and I needed to be careful if bending over, but it was perfectly acceptable for a spring barbecue.

"Well, Jim. She's your daughter," said Helen snidely. "Hattie you should put on a turtleneck to hide that awful hickey."

Of course my father didn't answer.

"Excuse me for a moment. I just need to run upstairs and grab something," I said.

As I began to walk away Helen made sure to call after me.

"Hurry up, there's a lot to do before guests arrive."

I ignored the woman, her spiky platinum blonde hair, and her fake pearls and continued on to my bedroom. I grabbed my phone from my dresser and flopped onto my bed with it. I turned it on and smiled when I saw Saul's face looking at me. I found his number in my contacts list and tapped the screen with my finger until I got to a blank text message. I began tapping at the on screen keyboard to send him a message of desperation.

Saul. Lina. Please hurry! Helen's here. She looks like an albino artichoke! Help! –Hattie

I rolled over onto my belly clutching the phone in my hand as if it were a last lifeline to my own sanity. It seemed an eternity before the phone chirped back at me. I rolled onto my back again and held the phone in front of my face. I tapped the screen until a new text message appeared.

Be there in two. Avoid spiky veggies. S & L

I took a deep breath, closed my eyes, and wished for a moment that I was back inside Saul's small house wrapped in his arms.

"Hattie, hurry up!" I heard Joe call up the stairs.

I groaned quietly to myself and force myself up off the bed and onto my feet. I cringed when I heard the grating sound of tires squealing and metal crunching from somewhere nearby. Keeping my phone in my hand, I reluctantly walked back downstairs and into artichoke danger zone.

"Ahhh, there she is! How are you, sweetie pie?" came Miranda's gentle voice.

"Thank God you're here! I was about bored to death," I said as I walked to her and quickly hugged her. "Helen's here," I whispered with dread in my voice.

"Be nice," she warned. "You look pretty, Hattie."

"Thank you," I said, followed by a quick smile.

"Everett's outside. I think he's asking Helen about her new hairdo."

I actually had to force myself to not laugh. "I'll go say hi in a minute."

"I'm glad you two are getting along again. You know I think of you as one of my own, right?"

I nodded. "The feelings mutual."

Miranda took hold of my hand and gave it a gentle squeeze, which was yet another reminder of how important she was to me. In the distance I could hear sirens.

"Hey, Hat."

"Hi," I said to Everett.

"Did you two hear that wreck?" he asked us.

"Yeah it sounded nasty," said his mom.

"It's just outside at the end of the block," he added.

A knock on the door caused my heart to speed up. I let go of Miranda's hand and practically ran to answer it, anxious to see Saul. As I swung my door inward, instead of being met with a warm spring breeze, the sight of Lina standing on the porch with blood dripping down her face made me go numb to my core.

"Lina? What the fuck…" I began to say.

Everett pushed me aside and pulled her into the living room. Blood dripped all over our carpet, but that was the least of my concerns.

"Lina! What happened?" The girl looked like she was in shock and stammered incoherently.

"Mom! Grab a towel and call 911," shouted Everett.

Lina, obviously about to collapse, was quickly gathered into Everett's arms; he rushed her to the couch, where he set her down carefully. Miranda hurried to his side, a kitchen towel in one hand and a cordless phone in the other.

"Carolina, where's your brother?" I asked, somewhat panicked. "Where's Saul? What happened?"

The front door had been left open and another siren rushed by, followed by the telltale deeper whoop of a fire engine. Everett gently put pressure on a wound on Lina's head, using the towel that Miranda had brought in.

"Saul," whimpered Lina.

I could hear deep voices coming from somewhere out front, and a woman shouting instructions of some kind.

"What's going on?" It was my father's voice.

I looked up at him as he entered the room.

"Good Lord Almighty, what happened? Oh my Lord she's getting blood all over the couch!" shrieked Helen in her stupid fake accent.

I stood on shaky legs and ran to the front door, leaving the house behind. I knew they would take care of Carolina, but right now I had to find Saul. I was sick to my stomach with worry. The driveway was filling with smoke and the horrible smell of burning oil and plastic. An ambulance was pulling up in front of our house. One of the medics was asking me who was injured.

"She's in here!" I heard Miranda yell to them from the front steps.

The street was a chaos of emergency vehicles, flashing red and blue lights, and mangled vehicles. A police officer tried to hold me back, but I forced my way past him to approach the wreck. Saul's truck was on its side; the hood badly caved in and shoved toward the cab. Glass and oil littered the street, along with bits of broken light covers and twisted pieces of metal. Steam or smoke was spiraling from a second vehicle, headed high into the late afternoon sky. I couldn't tell what the other vehicles make or model was, but I was quite sure it had been yellow. It was so crushed and twisted. As I got closer to the dangerous scene, arms encircled me and held me back. The thunderous roar of the Jaws of Life started at the same moment that my screams began.

On the far side of the road rested part of a human body. Whoever was holding me back, I allowed them to.

CHAPTER 15 ~ SLIPPING AWAY

The police officer who held me back could have been angry at me for fighting him, and likely was, but did his duty in keeping me safe. People were yelling all around me, their voices garbled by my own blood pounding in my ears and the sound of the machine ripping through the cab of Saul's truck. "Get her out of here!" and "Forget that one, he's dead!" were the only two coherent things I picked out of the jumble. The smoke was making it difficult to breathe and I didn't want to be drug away. I needed to get to Saul. I had to force myself to stay in the present, when it felt so much like I was back in the middle of the explosions.

"Stop!" I shouted as loud as I could muster, trying to break free.

"Hattie, no!" It was my father's voice. "Stop, it's not safe!"

In the distance I heard Miranda yelling at Helen. It was rare for Miranda to actually cuss. Something about it made me start laughing. I was back in the front yard now, my father and my brother on either side of me, holding my arms. I shrugged them off, but stayed where I was, watching the scene before us.

"Saul! Saul!" I screamed. "Oh God, Saul!" I could barely recognize my own voice through the sound of my own fear.

The ambulance crew was busy bringing Lina out from the house behind us, complete with a stretcher and neck brace. Her head had been bandaged and blood was wicking through. She was pale and her eyes full of terror.

"Lina!" I ran to her side, once there matching the pace of the moving stretcher. "What happened?"

"Hit us…" she muttered, along with something else that was incoherent.

"Lina, was Saul driving?" I pressed.

The traumatized girl began crying. "Where's Saul?" She was nearly hysterical and barely able to ask the question.

"You're going to have to step back now, ma'am; let us get her loaded and the hospital," said a slightly plump woman wearing tight navy blue slacks and a white uniform shirt that bore the logo of the ambulance company.

I obediently took a step back to let them do their job. Everett was standing behind me and put his hands on my shoulders. I found it comforting, albeit in the smallest of ways. Within the next moments Lina's ambulance backed out of our driveway and turned right. I watched it for only a brief moment before looking back to the accident scene. Other neighbors had gathered on their porches and in their yards and also looked on.

Flames had begun to erupt from the smaller mangled vehicle. One of the two fire engines had begun spraying water in an attempt to extinguish the fire. Three different firemen continued to work with the Jaws of Life, their efforts appearing to double now that active flames were present on the scene. As the metal cutters finally quieted I could hear one of the firemen shouting for the others to help move parts of the truck frame back. I put my hands over my mouth and waited.

At long last I saw one of the firefighters pull Saul from the wreckage. Everett, still standing behind me, encircled me in his arms. Things seemed surreal as I watched the medics carefully load Saul onto a stretcher. I didn't see any blood but I was also standing at a distance. Two of the medics fastened a long safety strap around his body as a third and fourth secured a brace around his neck. I knew he was alive because he raised one of his arms. I let out a sigh of relief and turned to face Everett. He held me close as I rested my cheek against his chest. He stroked my back soothingly.

"Hat, let's get you inside," said Everett.

"I need to go with him," I insisted.

My father had walked over to where we stood and placed a hand upon my shoulder. "No, let them work on him," he said. "We'll find out where they're taking him and meet them there in a little while."

I nodded, knowing that he was right. I let Everett take me back into the house. He guided me to the living room where we sat together on the couch. He kept an arm around my shoulders and I leaned against him.

"Carolina. Is she going to be okay?" I asked

Miranda walked over, carrying a glass of water and set it on the coffee table in front of me.

"The ambulance guys seem to think so. They're taking her into Anacortes for x-rays just to make sure her spine is okay and to stitch up the side of her head."

"Good. She's a really sweet girl," I said as I picked up the glass of water.

"She Saul's sister?" asked Everett.

After swallowing a sip of water I nodded. "Yeah, she just flew in from Virginia last night."

"Well she better pay to have this carpet cleaned," added Helen. I ignored her completely.

"Honey, your dad's seeing if he can find out where they took Saul and once we know one of us will drive you there," said Miranda sweetly.

"Thanks," I managed to mumble.

My stomach was in a knot and all of a sudden I felt exhausted. When my father entered the room talking on his cell phone, I sat up straighter. He held his index finger up, indicating that I should wait. I sat as patiently as I could and Everett took his arm from around my shoulders and slipped my hand into his.

Soon, my father was off of the phone and sat in the chair that was kiddy-corner to the couch.

"The crew outside was really busy but one of them said that they were pretty sure they were taking Saul to Anacortes General. That's a good thing, because if he were real bad off they'd be life flight'ing him to Harborview down in Seattle," said my father.

"Yeah, he's right, Hat," said Everett.

"I need to go see him."

"I'll take you. Just let me grab my keys," said Everett.

"Why don't the rest of us stay put and go ahead with the barbecue? That tiny hospital doesn't need all of us taking up space in the waiting room," said Miranda.

Joe and Justine were standing together near the threshold to the kitchen and he had an arm around her. I suddenly felt bad about leaving on their special day. Knowing me too well, Joe spoke up.

"Go, Hattie. Will be fine here."

I walked to him and gave him a quick hug and followed it with a kiss to Justine's cheek.

"Call as soon as you know something?" said my new sister-in-law.

I nodded. "I will."

***

The drive to Anacortes General was unremarkable. The sky had turned gray and the temperature had dropped. I was glad to have Everett at my side. We walked through the main entrance together and across a small lobby to a reception desk that was labeled "INFORMATION." A little elderly woman was behind the desk. She wore a dark blue smock and half-moon reading lessons. Her gray hair was just barely a hint of blue and she wore it in short curls. Her earlobes sagged from heavy sapphire earrings. She smiled at us as we approached, which caused her entire face to light up. As upset as I was, I found myself smiling back.

"How can I help you young lady, young man?" asked the charming older woman.

"I think my friends might have been brought here," I said in a shaky voice. "They were in a car wreck over on the edge of Fidalgo Bay."

"Ohhhh yessss," she said in an overly sympathetic grandmotherly voice. "I heard about that from some of our nurses. Let's take a look and see if your friends were admitted. What are their names, Honey?"

I felt Everett place his hands on my shoulders. It had a very calming effect.

"Saul and Carolina Meyers."

The woman tapped away at a keyboard. Her arthritic fingers were much faster than I would have imagined.

"Oh yes! I see them right here. They're both still in the emergency room."

"Can you point us in that direction, please?" asked Everett.

"I can give you a map if you'd like," offered the sweet little woman. "But it might make it more confusing."

"Thanks, we'll trust you," I said.

The woman flashed us another of her brilliant smiles. "Just take that escalator right there down one level. At the bottom turn left and keep going straight. Once you can't go anymore, you're at the emergency room. Just go in through the red double doors and the nurses station is right there and they'll help you out. Tell them Mrs. Carole sent you."

"Thanks, ma'am," said Everett. "We appreciate it."

"You're welcome. And I hope your friends feel better real soon."

"Thanks," I said quickly, anxious to get to Saul's side.

Everett took my hand in his and we walked to the escalator together. I could feel my anxiety growing as we walked down the moving steps, surpassing the automated speed.

"He'll be okay, Hat."

I looked over at Everett. "You think so?"

"I hope so."

"Thanks, Ev."

The hallways were painted a neutral tan color and the floors were an off-white tile that had little blue speckles in the pattern. It all felt very cold. An occasional framed print hung on the walls, but they did little to make it feel warm or welcoming.

"That's it up there," I said when I saw the red doors.

I quickened my pace, pulling Everett along with me. The doors swung inward easily enough. I had expected a lot of noise once we were in the emergency room, but it was oddly quiet. There were a handful of red plastic seats, but only three were occupied. Just as promised, a nurse's station was in plain view. A clean-cut black man who looked to be perhaps in his forties sat in a chair behind the desk looking at a computer screen, seemingly lost in his own world. He wore blue scrubs and a name badge clipped to a front shirt pocket that read "David K."

After we had waited for several seconds, the man finally looked up.

"Can I help you?" he asked, his voice gentle and soothing.

"We're looking for Saul and Carolina Meyers. They were brought in after a bad car accident," I said quickly.

"Just a moment while I look them up," said the man. His fingers clicked away at the keyboard and within a moment he looked up. "They're both here. I can show you where Carolina is, but it looks like Saul is in radiology."

"Thank you," I said.

The man stood and we followed him around the desk and through a threshold that lead to a larger room that was sectioned off into cubicles. Each smaller room had a panel of cloth for privacy that hung from tracks in the ceiling.

"She's just down at the end of this row," he explained.

Most of the little rooms were obviously empty, but four had lights on with the privacy curtains drawn. I heard someone cough loudly; the kind of hacking cough that grates on your nerves. By the sound, I guessed it was an old man. Finally, the man escorting us stopped at the last cubicle on our right. He knocked on the wall that was beside the privacy curtain.

"Miss Meyers, is it okay to send a couple of visitors in?"

"Sure, David. Thank you."

The sound of Lina's voice made my heart skip a beat; I was just so happy to hear her.

"You two go on in. But make sure you let her get some rest." The man winked at me before walking away.

Everett quietly held the curtain back and I stepped into the cubicle. A huge smile spread across Lina's face. Her left cheek was bruised and swollen, causing her grin to be a bit lopsided. Her left eye was almost swelled shut and she had a bandage on her right temple. I smiled back at her, not sure just what I should say.

"Dang girl, that's some shiner you've got!" said Everett, sounding a bit like a fool.

"Attractive, huh?" she said back to him.

"Lina, I'm so glad you're okay," I whispered as I walked to her side.

She patted the mattress beside her, indicating that I should sit down. I did so, but reluctantly; I didn't want to do anything that might hurt her. Everett remained standing, his arms across his chest, and leaned against the wall by the foot of her bed.

"Have you seen Saul yet?" she asked.

I shook my head side to side. "Not yet."

"Have you heard anything about him?" she pressed.

Everett shifted his weight to his other foot. "Just that he's here."

"They told me that they took him for a CT scan just to make sure his neck is okay. The doctor who first saw me said were lucky to both still be alive and that it's a miracle we don't seem to have any major injuries." Lina's entire face lit up as she began laughing. "You should have heard him after they gave him a shot of pain medicine! Oh my God! He was laughing at the stupidest things."

Suddenly Lina's happy expression turned to one of grief.

Everett walked to her and took one of her hands in his.

"Hey now, what's wrong?"

The girl sniffled and wiped away a fresh tear that had begun to fall down her cheek.

"I heard the nurses talking. The other driver died."

I nodded and gently took her other hand in my own, being careful of the IV line in her arm.

"Yeah, they did. Lina, do you know what happened?" I asked.

"Saul was driving. He had driven by your house once to show me where it was. He offered to let me out while he parked farther down the street." She took a deep breath before continuing. "I told him no, that I would go with him. If I would've said yes maybe none of this would've happened."

"Nah," said Everett. "You can't be thinking like that."

Lina had been staring at her lap but looked up at him and nodded slightly.

"He drove around the block one more time since there weren't any spots big enough for his truck on your street. He headed back and as we drove into the intersection...well, I don't remember much after that."

"Do you remember walking to my house?" I asked.

"No. I actually don't. The doctor said that things might be a little fuzzy for a while. She even said I might not remember today or tomorrow because of pain medication they're giving me."

"Cool," said Everett, who flashed her a goofy grin.

"Not so much," she said in a tired voice.

A girl dressed in scrubs walked into the cubicle. She couldn't have been any older than myself or Everett, and was slender with long blonde hair. I was surprised that Everett didn't trip over himself trying to impress her.

"Carolina?" asked the pretty nurse.

Lina nodded in reply. "That's me."

"I brought you one more shot of pain medicine before we get you started onto pills. The doc says you can go home in about an hour."

Lina looked panicked. "I'm just visiting town. I'm staying with my brother and he's here too."

"Do you have any other family in town? Or friends you can stay with?"

Lina shook her head, looking like someone had just kicked her dog.

"I can order the social services consult. It might buy you a few more hours."

I let go of Lina's hand and stood beside the bed. "She can stay with me," I said without hesitation.

"Hattie, that's really sweet but you've only known me for a day."

"Well. That'll just have to be long enough," said Everett.

The nurse walked to Lina's side, doing her best to work around Everett. She looked carefully at the ID band on Lina's wrist, looked over her IV tubing, and eventually prepared a syringe of medication.

"Carolina, can you tell me what your date of birth is?" asked the girl.

"Yeah. October thirty-first, 1983."

"Thanks. And on a scale of one to ten, how bad is your headache?"

"Maybe a six?"

"Okay, thanks. I' going to give you some morphine. After this dose we'll give you something to eat and start you on pain pills. You can leave after that, as long as your friends promise to stay with you for the next twenty-four hours to watch for signs of a concussion?"

The nurse slowly injected the medication into the IV line.

"You'll get sleepy from this, Carolina. Take advantage of it and sleep," suggested the young nurse.

Within seconds of the nurse finishing, Lina's eyes got droopy. Before long she was snoring softly. The blonde nurse used the button on Lina's bedrail to flatten the head of her bed so that she was lying down.

"She'll probably sleep for an hour or two," said the nurse.

"Do you know where her brother is?" I asked.

"Oh, yeah, the funny guy. They just brought him back from radiology."

"Can we see him?"

"Sure. I'll show you to his little room."

"Hat, I'm gonna wait in the lobby," said Everett.

I smiled at him. "Thanks. If you want to go back home I can figure out how to get Lina home later."

"Nah, I'll camp out here till you're both ready to leave."

"If you're hungry, the cafeteria's open for another hour," said the nurse. I couldn't quite tell if she was inviting him or just telling him.

"Thanks," was all he said in reply. He seemed absolutely clueless that the nurse obviously had the hots for him.

"Okay then. I'll show you to Mr. Meyers' room."

I followed the nurse out to the common area and across the room to another cubicle. She didn't say anymore and Everett went the opposite direction to wait in the lobby.

"Mr. Meyers, you okay with a visitor?" she asked through Saul's privacy curtain.

"As long as it's not that mean nurse from earlier," I heard him call out, followed by a chuckle.

I didn't wait for the official 'come in,' but rather slid past the edge of the curtain until I was in the room.

"My Angel," he said once he saw me.

I smiled softly. "Hey."

"Hey," he whispered back.

"You okay?" I could hear the trepidation in my own voice.

"I'll be okay, sweet thing. Just a little sore."

He held an arm out for me, and I gladly walked to his side.

"Saul, I was so afraid I'd lost you."

I sat on the edge of the bed and leaned against him cautiously. He wrapped an arm around me and kissed the top of my head.

"You still smell like sunshine and honey," he whispered.

"What happened?" I moaned into his chest, doing my best to keep my composure as the reality of the day was beginning to set in.

"Someone broadsided us. They ran right through the stop sign; fucking going way too goddamn fast."

"They died, Saul. The other driver."

I backed away from his chest to look at him.

He nodded silently at first. He moved a hand to my face and stroked my cheek with his thumb. "I know. Lina told me."

"I know we've only known each other for a few days," I said quietly. "But when I thought you were dead, it was like someone had taken my breath away. It was like life wasn't worth living."

He put his palm on the back of my head and gently pulled my head back to his chest.

"I think I know how you feel," he said. "It's kind-of like I've know you for most of my life, Hattie. I mean that's how it feels. I'll be honest. When I was stuck in my truck and they were using that damned machine to cut me out, all I could think about was if I'd see you again. That's all I wanted, was to see your face again. To hold you."

I sighed, melting into him a bit. His voice got really quiet, but I heard him loud and clear.

"I love you, Hattie."

It was the first time I had heard those words from a man other than my own brother or my father.

Somehow, the words felt natural and they felt real; they felt right.

"I love you too," I said, not hesitating to utter the words. They felt as right to say as they had to hear.

I kept my head against his chest, but looked up to meet his eyes. He smiled at me and I felt almost complete. Almost.

CHAPTER 16 ~ DRIFT WOOD

Almost a week had passed and Saul and Lina had both mended, for the most part. Everett and I had taken them back to Saul's little house, where I had tended to both of them for a couple of days. Lina had been called back to Virginia to give a statement on the death of the family for which she had nannied. Saul had suffered a hairline fracture of one of his ribs, which was beginning to heal by now. We spent most of our time watching movies and laying around. We were both getting cabin fever and ready to get out of the house.

Saul swore that he was up to some physical activity, so I talked him into a short walk at the beach. We had set out on foot, headed just three blocks to a small public park that sat water-side. We walked hand-in-hand.

"If you walk any faster you might pop your rib," I joked. "What me to carry you down the steps?" I laughed.

"I'd kind of like to see you try."

We began descending a set of timbers that created a stairway down to the rocky shore. The tide was high and the water calm; small but constant waves lapped at the shore.

"Do you want to go sit on that drift wood?" he asked me.

I looked at the path that led to a large log on the beach. "It looks too unstable," I answered.

He squeezed my hand and looked over at me. "I'm okay. I promise. It might be fun."

"Anything with you is fun, Saul. Well, except explosions and car wrecks."

We walked the short distance to a large log that had drifted in from Puget Sound and found a somewhat flat spot upon which to sit. A gentle breeze was blowing and in the distance I could hear the barking of a sea lion. There was new warmth to the air; a sure sign that summer was near.

Saul took a deep breath and cleared his throat. "The funerals tomorrow. I was hoping you'd go with me, but I understand if it's too painful."

"You're going to the funeral of the guy who ran into you guys?" I asked, surprised.

"No, no. The baby."

"Oh." I hung my head in thought.

"I just, I dunno, I just need to be there," he said somberly.

"Yeah. Of course I'll go with. What time?"

"Four o'clock."

"You're feeling strong enough to go?" I asked.

He patted his uninjured side. "Fit as a fiddle."

"Neither of us has a car," I mentioned the obvious.

"We better get one, then," he said with a smile.

"We?" I repeated.

"Sure. We can share it."

I laughed. "You're weird."

"So I'm told. There's something else I want to talk to you about."

"Uh-oh. Did I do something wrong?" I felt instantly crushed, figuring he was about to tell me to take a hike.

"No, no. Of course not. You're awesome in so many ways. This is kind-of a weird one to bring up. I mean I know we've only been together for what, a week and a half?"

"Almost two," I added.

"We haven't really talked much about our plans. About where we want things to go from here."

"I guess I've just kinda been going with it. It's new to me, Saul. I'm not sure how to act or what to say half the time."

"Well, you being you is a great start. 'Cause I kind of sort of like you a whole lot, if you haven't noticed." He reached down and took my hand in his.

"So what's up? You want to talk about the 'what's next'?"

"You've been spending a lot of time at my place. I thought maybe we could make that a little more permanent."

I looked at him, a bit confused. "Like me leaving a toothbrush there?"

He laughed at me, causing his eyes to brighten. "Well, maybe a toothbrush and some clothes and the rest of your stuff. I want you to move in, Hattie. Come live with me."

I squinted my eyes at him. I wasn't sure if I should laugh or cry.

"Are you serious?" I asked, not quite sure if he was joking or not.

"Very. If you need time to think about it, I understand. I know it's really soon to bring it up."

He leaned forward slowly, still guarding his side, and kissed me gently on the lips. My stomach did a flip-flop and I returned his kiss eagerly.

"I don't need time to think."

"Is that a no, then?"

I smiled at him. "No, that's a yes. I'll move in with you."

He grinned like a little boy in a Lego store. "When?"

"Whoa boy, calm down! We should talk about a few things first," I said with a slight chuckle. "I'm going to need to look for a job soon. I'll want to at least pay for part of utilities and groceries."

"That's fair enough, but please don't be in a rush. My granddad left me a hefty sum. If you want to work that's totally fine, but maybe it would be good to take some time off? Maybe we could go somewhere for a few days?"

I was wearing a pleated plaid skirt that, when standing, only fell to just above my knees. I blushed when I felt his warm hand slide up my bare thigh.

"You're trying to distract me," I said as I felt my insides tingle with longing.

"Uh-huh," he groaned softly near my ear. His hand traveled to my inner thigh, causing me to gasp quietly.

"You're driving me crazy," I moaned as I felt one of his fingers slide beneath my panties.

"Good," he whispered just before he started gently sucking on my neck.

As his finger began gently searching, my legs automatically parted just a bit hoping it would help him find his way inside of me.

"Saul, someone might see us."

I whimpered as his finger found its mark and entered me deeply.

"Oh God, Hattie. Your pussy's so wet."

He began stroking me on the inside, growling against my neck. I opened my legs farther and adjusted my hips in hopes that he would go deeper.

"Fuck," I whimpered pathetically. "Oh God, I want you inside of me, Saul."

To my dismay, he slid his finger from me. I watched as he slowly put it into his mouth.

"You taste so good," he said under his breath. I wasn't sure if I should be embarrassed or turned on.

"Make you a deal," I said.

"What kind?"

"I'll start moving in tomorrow but only if you take me home and make love to me. Hard."

"Let's go," he said as he stood.

***

It hadn't taken as long to walk back to his house since we were both in a hurry. The temperature had started to drop as evening approached. The little house felt cool but neither of us could be bothered to start a fire.

"Okay, sweet thing. You have me so fucking horny," he said as soon as we walked in the front door.

As the door shut behind us he gently grabbed onto both sides of my head and began kissing me with passion. He twisted my hair around his fingers and pressed against me with his hard cock.

"Will you do me one favor?" he asked while looking me in the eyes.

"Right now I'd do just about anything to feel you inside of me."

"Keep the skirt on? It's super sexy."

"Uh-huh. Sure," I whispered as I pulled off my white T-shirt, leaving just my brazier.

"It's a pretty bra, but it can go," he said as he devoured me with his eyes.

He got closer and wrapped his arms around me while he began tasting my neck again. Expertly, he unfastened the back of my bra and his hands moved to my shoulders. He wound his fingers beneath the straps and slid them down my arms. His gaze fell to my bare chest. My nipples were erect from the cold and excitement and he groaned as he took in the sight.

"God you're gorgeous, Hattie Cakes."

He used to the pad of his thumb to lightly stroke one of my nipples. I reached out and slid my own hands up the front of his T-shirt, enjoying the feel of his hard abs while being careful to not hurt his injured rib. He took my cue and pulled his shirt up and over his head. His smooth, muscular chest was gorgeous and made me want him that much more. Wearing only jeans, he knelt down and reached both hands up my skirt. He leaned forward and nuzzled his face against the plaid fabric. His breath felt hot between my legs, causing me to moan in anticipation of what was to come. He kept his face against me while reaching his hands around to my backside. His grip on me was firm and his obvious desire drove me wild. I ran my hands over the top of his head, grabbing onto his hair and pulling gently. Hooking his thumbs into the top band of my panties, he finally slid them down and they fell softly to the floor. I could feel my own wetness and was more than ready to have him inside of me.

"Bedroom?" he asked softly as he gazed up into my eyes.

I nodded, not breaking his gaze. He stood and took hold of one of my hands and guided me to the back room. I was nude now, aside from my silly pleated school-girl skirt, and I had never been more turned on. We walked to the side of the bed together, where he faced me while the backs of my legs touched the mattress.

"Sit for a minute?" he suggested.

I sat on the edge of the bed, watching him. He began to unzip his jeans, never taking his eyes off of me. I leaned back on my hands, waiting. He slid his jeans and boxers down at the same time, freeing his erection. I scooted back on the bed and situated myself until I was sitting up against the headboard. Saul walked, naked, to his dresser. His ass was tight and I loved the way he moved. He opened the top drawer and soon I heard the telltale sound of a condom package being opened. He walked back to the bed and sat on the edge next to me, halfway turned toward me.

"Do you still want me to make love to you?" he asked quietly while he unrolled the condom onto his hard cock.

I licked my lips and nodded. He turned and climbed on top of me, kissing me deeply while reaching beneath my skirt with one of his hands. His fingers searched until he found the moist warmth that was spilling past my lips. He traced lightly with his fingertips, making me shudder in delight.

I could feel Saul's breath against my neck as he whispered to me. "I'm so hard for you, Hattie."

I took his face in my hands and found his mouth with mine. The angle of his jaw felt strong beneath my palms and my insides were on fire with desire. I squirmed beneath him, getting his attention.

"Is it ok if I'm on top this time?" I asked very quietly. "I've just always wondered what it's like," I began to explain, suddenly slightly embarrassed.

"Just promise to not press down on my ribs and you can ride me whichever way you want," he said with a shit-eating grin.

"Will you tell me what to do?" I asked somewhat sheepishly.

He carefully rolled off of me, situating himself near the center of the bed. I looked over the length of his body. He was lean and muscular, and his cock was erect and waiting for me. I stood on my knees on the mattress beside him and he reached up to caress one of my bare breasts while I began to straddle him. I adjusted my skirt until it was out of the way in the front and slyly looked at him.

"What should I do next?" I asked, pretending I was clueless.

"Oh God, girl, you're driving me crazy. I need to fuck you so bad."

I took his cock in my hand and pretended to look at it with only half interest. I leaned back just a bit, putting my weight on his thighs, and gently placed his shaft against myself. He moaned in frustration. Finally, I lifted my hips just enough to guide him in to me. I let the head of his penis sit at my opening for a painful moment before finally lowering myself down until he filled me. His back arched and he groaned in pleasure. He held his hands up for me to take hold of, which was useful in protecting his broken rib. I began moving my hips in earnest, allowing myself to slide up and down as he worked at thrusting with his own rhythm. The sensation was different than what I had known before, the grinding on my clit sending me into a wave of pleasure far beyond what he had shown me so far. Not long after, he too found his release with a loudness he hadn't shared the other times we had been together. I leaned down and placed my forehead against his chest, still being careful to not hurt him. We stayed like that for several moments before I gently climbed off and lay down.

"Thank you," he whispered.

"Was it okay?"

He chuckled. "Much more than okay."

I heard him climb out of bed and watched as he walked to the bathroom. I slid my skirt off and climbed under the covers. The room was cold and I was exhausted.

Just as I was beginning to doze off, Saul's deep voice woke me.

"Ready for bed?"

I nodded. "I'm so tired."

"I'll turn out the lights. Tomorrow's a big day."

I closed my eyes and waited for him to climb in beside me. Once he did, I snuggled up to him hoping to borrow some of his body heat.

"Saul?" I mumbled sleepily.

"Hmm?"

"I started birth control while you were in the hospital. We'll be safe in a few more days."

I felt him kiss my forehead. "Thanks," he whispered. "I love you."

"Me too."

CHAPTER 17 ~ PLANS

When I woke, I wasn't sure where I was. My lungs burned and my skin felt hot. I could hear the commotion from the explosion around me, but it was muffled. I gasped for breath.

"Easy there," said Saul, his deep voice grounding me.

I continued to struggle for air.

"Hattie, you're ok. I think you had another bad dream."

"I was there," I whimpered. "Back at the explosion. So many people were yelling."

"It's okay," he reassured me.

I was sitting upright. Trying to get my bearings. I felt his warm hand on my back. The images that my mind had woven while I slept were thankfully fading, but an ominous feeling had been left behind.

"Do you mind getting me some water?" I asked.

He kissed my temple. "Sure. Of course."

The room was lightening with daylight and I wondered what time it was. I listened as Saul eased his way out of the bed and walked in the dark to the bathroom in the hallway. Some moments later the toilet flushed and I heard him rummaging through the kitchen. My heartbeat was finally starting to slow back down to something resembling normalcy. My bladder was telling me to get out of bed, the cold was telling me to stay in, and nothing was telling me to go back to sleep. I sighed heavily and finally crawled out of the warm bed.

On the way to the bathroom, I quickly turned on the lamp that Saul kept on the dresser and rummaged through his drawers until I found a t-shirt to borrow. Once semi-dressed, I made my way to the bathroom, and eventually to the kitchen. Saul stood there in boxer shorts making coffee, which had already begun to brew. It smelled heavenly.

"I heard you get up," he said as he took two empty mugs from a cabinet and set them on the counter.

"I don't think I can go back to sleep," I admitted. "What time is it?"

"Eight o'clock. Hey, nice shirt."

I smiled. "Hope you don't mind?"

"Of course not. It's today now. Your home, including all that's in it. Me. And my shirts."

"I'll need to talk to Joe and Justine later this morning. They might like the idea of me moving out. Making room for the baby and all."

"You sure you're ready for this?" he asked. "Living with me?"

"It's fast, but I know it feels right."

I watched as he opened the freezer and took out a half-gallon of Breyer's vanilla bean ice cream. He carefully put a scoop into each mug before putting it away.

"What are you doing?" I asked, wondering what kind of a goofball I had gotten myself involved with.

"Oh, it's an age-old recipe to cure nightmare hangovers," he said as he winked at me.

"You're so weird," I said with a slight chuckle.

"Seriously. My mom used to make this for us anytime we'd wake up and couldn't go back to sleep.

Well, back then it was vanilla ice cream with hot cocoa. This version is better."

"Sounds…interesting."

"I have a Presto log ready to light in the fireplace. We can have our coffee in there. Talk for a while if you want?"

I nodded. "Okay. Tell me where the lighter is and I'll go start the log? I'm freezing."

"It's one of those wand things; on the mantle."

"Saul?"

"Hmm?"

"Thanks."

"Anytime, babe."

I slowly wandered into the living room. The lighter was right where he had said to expect it and soon the Presto log was afire. As if on cue, Saul walked in with two mugs of coffee. I took mine from him gratefully and held it in both hands, taking advantage of the warmth of the mug.

"Here, hold mine for a sec?" he asked, holding his mug out for me.

I took it without question and watched as he spread a quilt over the couch for us. I sat carefully, still holding both mugs, and smiled when he covered me with an afghan. Once he sat beside me, I handed him his coffee and finally sipped at mine. It was a lot better than I had imagined; it was almost sinful.

"You like it, don't you?" he asked.

"It's really good."

"So, tell me something. Have you been having nightmares every night?"

"Pretty much."

"It's a lot to cope with. Maybe getting away for a break would be good after all."

I looked at him sideways while taking another sip of sinfulness. "I can't afford a vacation."

"Then let me take you."

"That'd feel weird."

"It shouldn't. I'm not working right now. I have extra money. Let me take you away for a few days."

"I'll think about it. But no promises. Hey, I need to grab some clothes from home for the funeral today; assuming you still want to go?"

"I'd like to. Actually, no, I *need* to be there," he said somberly.

I set my free hand on his thigh and squeezed. "Then I'll be there with you."

The telltale ring of Saul's cell phone went off; "I'm Too Sexy for my Shirt." He had told me that Lina had programmed that in over a year ago. It made me wonder how she was getting along back on the East Coast.

I watched as Saul stood by the small front window, facing away from me, and listened in idly while he spoke.

"Yup this morning at ten works perfect. Actually sooner is fine too. Uh-huh. I'll be here. Oh, make sure the tank's full?"

Once he hung up, he returned to his seat next to me on the couch and leaned his head back.

"You look tired," I said while I stroked a few stray strands of hair away from his brow.

"It's been hectic lately."

"That's an understatement."

"That was my car insurance contact. They're delivering a new truck today."

"Already?" I asked, surprised.

"Yeah, pretty quick huh? It's not brand new, but close to it. A little smaller than the old one. But heck, it'll do and then there's some cash left over."

"That's cool."

"Makes me glad I paid for gap insurance. I still owed on the Ford, so they paid that off, let me buy the used one, and I get the difference in a nice check."

"Sweet."

"Good timing too. We can use the new rig to move some of your stuff."

"I won't have much, really. Just clothes and bathroom stuff, and a few odds-n-ends."

"No furniture?"

Not unless you want me to bring some? I'm sure Joe and Justine can use what's there. I love my bed but if they want it they can use it."

I looked at him sideways and smiled.

"Well, I guess you can sleep in my bed if you want." He winked, letting me know he was being sarcastic.

"I should get home. Pack a few things and get ready for the funeral."

"Hattie?" His tone changed, his deep voice sounding very serious.

"Hmm?"

"Go to Hawaii with me?"

I laughed. "I can't afford a trip like that, Saul. Otherwise it sounds nice."

"My feelings are hurt," he said with a pout on his face. "Let me take you?"

I adjusted myself on the sofa, turning to face him. I reached over and set my coffee cup on the little table in front of the couch. Twisting to face me, he mirrored me. I reached a hand out and found his, and laced my fingers though his.

"It's too much," I said with sincerity in my voice.

"Then we'll go for just half the time."

I wanted to laugh, but his face was too serious. His eyes were looking at me, their depth reflecting some desire deep within.

"Saul…"

He held his index finger up to my lips to quiet me. He let it linger there, and I closed my eyes for a moment. I felt his hand tighten around my own, but kept my eyes closed. His touch made me feel whole.

"Hattie, look at me." His voice had deepened, and his words had been said so very quietly.

I opened my eyes as he took his finger from my lips. He had leaned forward almost imperceptibly and took my other hand in his. I looked at him without saying anything.

"Come to Hawaii with me?"

The connection I felt with him at that moment was indescribable. I simply nodded 'yes.'

"Marry me."

I blinked. A few times. I wasn't quite sure I had heard him right and was about to ask him what he had said when he repeated it.

"Marry me."

"Saul…" I wasn't sure what to say. "That's not funny."

His face remained serious with no hint of joking.

"I mean it, Hattie. I want you to marry me."

"We just met," I whispered. "How can you say that?"

He took a deep breath and leaned back, still holding my hands in his. He never stopped looking directly at me. "I know it sounds crazy, but since we met I haven't stopped thinking about you. It's hard to think about anything else; like it's hard to breathe when you're not close to me. I can't imagine life without you. I know we barely know each other, but I swear if you say yes I'll be the best husband I can be. And a good father, if you want kids some day?"

I let go of his hands and stood, needing a minute to process what all he had just said. I could hear him shifting his body on the couch. I walked to the front window and looked out. The sky was beginning to cloud over and darken. It would be fitting for a funeral.

"Looks like it might rain," I said without much emotion.

I turned to face Saul again. He was situated on the edge of the couch, arms on his knees, just watching me. He looked a bit nervous. I crossed my arms over my chest and turned back to the window.

"Why me?" I asked quietly, not particularly expecting an answer.

"If you ask me, it was just meant to be. I've never felt like this about anyone before."

"What if time passes and you decide I'm annoying?"

I heard him stand and walk toward me. I stayed facing the window and waited. Soon, his warm arms wrapped around me. I felt the scruff of his face nestle against my neck.

"I'm sorry if the question scared you. I'll be honest. I didn't mean to ask you like that. I would have done it over a romantic dinner or something. But I've never been more serious about anything in my life. I want you, all of you, and I want you forever. I want to love you, to take care of you, and to grow old with you."

I wriggled in his arms until I was facing him. "You're really serious?"

He nodded. "I am."

"Can I take some time to think about it?"

"Hattie. I'll wait as long as it takes."

"Okay. I'll go."

"To Hawaii?"

I nodded.

"But I need some time to think about the rest of it."

"I'll wait," he whispered just before his soft lips brushed against mine. "Forever if I have to."

Chapter 18 ~ SAYING GOODBYE

Saul's new truck was supposed to be black like the old one, but a mix-up had left him as the new owner of a cherry red crew-cab with really big wheels. He grumbled about it for several minutes and had a heated conversation with the insurance rep before giving in and coming to terms with his new ride. I had never really heard him angry before, other than the brief outburst where he tried to kill the dumpster as we drove away from the explosion and the night of Joe's wedding when Everett got out of line toward me. I wasn't quite sure how to handle his mood, so did my best to blend in with the furniture while he worked it out. He growled to himself after he hung up his phone and I forced myself to not giggle. The truth was he was sexy when angry and I was pretty turned on.

By the time he joined me in the living room, his hair was mussed from him grabbing at it and his shirt was untucked. "Fucking insurance company," he grumbled.

"It's a pretty truck," I said quietly, testing out his mood.

"You like it?" he asked, his demeanor softening a touch.

I nodded and stood, walking toward him. "I do."

"Then you can have it," he said, smirking.

"You can't give me a truck." I reached my hands up and began unbuttoning his wrinkled shirt.

"But you can give me a shower."

"You're trying to distract me, aren't you?"

I smiled slyly. "Is it working?"

"Uh-huh."

I had unbuttoned all but the bottom button of his shirt, which I was now struggling with. He covered my hands with his own and worked his strong fingers until the task was done. I placed my palms against his strong abs and slowly moved up to his muscular chest. I could hear his breathing deepen under my touch. He leaned down to kiss me and I moved my hands to his bare shoulders and eventually guided his shirt down his arms. Our kiss deepened and his tongue worked feverishly to taste me.

"I want to you so bad," he whispered against my neck as he ran his hands up my shirt.

With a new-found sense of urgency, I pulled my shirt off and Saul helped free me of my bra. We worked our way out of the rest of our clothes and set off on our way to the bathroom. Once there, Saul turned on the hot water and while it warmed he guided me to a place against the wall. He moved forward and pressed himself against me. He had me pinned, holding my arms over my head with one of his strong hands. I could sense that he meant to take control when he smiled at me mischievously. The thought excited me greatly. Our eyes locked on each other for a brief moment before he kissed me deeply. I felt one of his hands slide down my bare side while the other kept my arms over my head. In the cold bathroom, the sensation was electric. My breathing deepened and became a bit irregular when his hand went from my hip to between my legs. His fingers began to gently slide inside of me, causing me to moan softly.

"How can you always be so ready for me?" he asked.

"Because you drive me crazy," I replied.

"Please say yes, Hattie?" he whispered with desperation in his voice. "Please. I can't live without you."

As badly as I wanted to shout the word 'yes' I knew that I had to have time to think. I gasped when his fingers left me and found my clit. His touch was so soft and gentle that I was amazed it could bring so much pleasure.

"When did you say we'd be safe with your birth control?" he asked.

"The doctor said in a week. It's been six days."

"Fuck," he grumbled against my neck. "I want to feel you so badly."

Suddenly he lifted me off of the floor so that I was straddling him. I locked my ankles together behind his back as he carried me to the shower. He looked at me tenderly as he tested the water and adjusted it slightly.

"Six days is almost a week," I said. "Tomorrow?"

He carried me into the shower. Still holding onto me, he rested my back against the tile wall. His face was pained with frustration.

"Do you have condoms in the shower?" I asked, nearly out of breath.

"No but we won't be in here long," he said as he resumed kissing me, his tongue hot and searching. "Think you can wait a few minutes or should we just head to the bedroom now?"

"Bedroom. Definitely," I breathed against his rugged cheek.

He held me to him and carried me out of the shower, leaving the water running. I clung to him as he carried me down the hallway. His erection was painfully close to where I longed for it to be, and I whimpered in frustration as the trip to his bed took too long for my liking.

"Almost there," he whispered.

A moment later he laid me on the bed. We were both still wet from the shower that we had abandoned, but I didn't care. I watched Saul as he went through his routine of rolling a condom over his hard shaft. Daringly, I used my own hand to start pleasuring myself. When he saw this, he grinned.

"That's a beautiful sight," he grumbled as he joined me on the bed. "But do you mind if I take over now?"

I bit my lower lip and shook my head slowly side to side. His wet hair dripped onto my chest as he mounted me and slowly opened me with his erection. I groaned as he filled me and began thrusting rhythmically. In a matter of a few minutes he took me to a place of such intense pleasure that all I could focus on was myself falling apart in his arms. He joined me in ecstasy as we came together. As he rolled off of me and onto his side, trying to catch his breath, I clung to him and sobbed into his chest.

"Shhhh," he soothed. "Hattie, what's wrong?"

"Nothing," I whimpered.

"That's not nothing, sweet thing. Talk to me."

"It's just not fair," I said through tears. "That we're here…when so many died."

I felt him take a deep breath as he backed away from me a few inches.

"I have no words, love. I wish I did. It's just going to take time. I'm glad we're both still here; alive. But I wish no one had died." His thumb wiped a tear from my cheek. "If you want we can skip the funeral today."

I shook my head. "No. We need to go. I'll be okay as long as you're there beside me."

"We'll leave in a few days. I'll schedule the plane tickets and a book a room. We'll work through this all together, okay?"

I nodded.

***

I had suggested that I drive Saul's truck home to prepare for the funeral, but he insisted on driving me until he trusted the vehicle. I hadn't argued. It was one o'clock already and he was due to pick me up at two. The funeral would be in Fidalgo Bay. Joe had told me he heard on the news that a large crowd was expected. He and Justine were planning to go and offered to escort me, but I politely declined. They settled for my agreeing to go out to dinner with them afterward. It would give me a chance to discuss my plans to move with them. My father and Helen were in Seattle for the day, thankfully.

Saul and I had finally made it to the shower together after making love, so all I needed to do was change into something appropriate for pay my respects. I chose a simple sleeveless dark brown dress that hugged my figure and fell just above my knees. I quickly French braided my hair and slipped on some simple pearl earrings and a matching necklace that had belonged to my mother. It was one of the only things of hers that I owned. While I had never truly met her and had no memories of her, the jewelry often comforted me when

I needed them. My father had given them to me on my tenth birthday, figuring I was responsible enough by then. It was the same year I had gotten my ears pierced. It was BH; "before Helen." I finished off the outfit with a very simple pair of brown pumps and a matching clutch in which to carry a handkerchief and my lip gloss. I didn't bother with makeup, knowing if I cried it would just smear.

By the time I was done I had twenty minutes left, so joined Justine for a cup of tea in the kitchen. I noticed an apartment guide sitting on the counter but decided to not ask about it. She was dressed in black slacks and a dark gray maternity shirt. Her bump was just beginning to show and she was glowing. We talked about some of their baby name ideas; they were favoring Iris for a girl and William for a boy. They weren't planning to find out gender until the baby was born. She was clearly excited as all get out.

***

Saul arrived at two o'clock sharp. Joe and Justine followed us to the funeral home. Since parking was packed, Saul and Joe parked several blocks away after dropping me and Justine off at the front door, where we waited for both men to return. I suspected that Joe wanted to talk to Saul alone, playing the role of protective brother.

People streamed past us into the funeral parlor. We were thirty minutes early, and the building was already nearly packed. Just as I thought to ask Justine if we should go find seats, Joe and Saul arrived. The four of us joined the other mourners who were walking inside. Flowers filled one side of the lobby, left by random citizens, family, and friends. There was a large banner that came from the local elementary school and had been decorated and signed by staff and students. I stood reading the banner just long enough to realize the mother of the baby had been a teacher there, out on maternity leave. I did my best to hold it together.

"Hattie, we need to sit," whispered Saul.

I held onto the crook of his arm and glanced at him absently. As we began walking, I realized we were following a man in a suit. I sensed Joe and Justine directly behind us. Saul led me around the main seating, following the usher. We were seated in a nearly empty section off to one side in an alcove. The lighting was dim and Saul whispered to me that the family had requested we be seated in the 'VIP' section. I looked across the main seating area and saw that an identical seating section mirrored us. Sitting there was an older couple and a man about ten years or so older than us. Sitting beside him and leaning against him was a young girl of about four years old. Her father held her hand tightly and she looked so very sad. They all had red-rimmed eyes with blank stares. I glanced to my left toward the front of the room and my heart sank when I saw a tiny white coffin surrounded by mounds of flowers, all in shades of ivory and white. Lilies, roses, daisies, carnations, and lots of baby's breath. Off to one side was a small table, covered in white lace, which held an eight-by-ten photograph of a mother and her infant as well as a small folded baby blanket. I took a deep breath, wanting to look away, but unable. Saul took my hand in his and squeezed lightly, breaking my trance. I looked over at him and his face calmed me. Soon others joined us on the pews upon which we sat. Most were in uniform: police, fire, EMT's. I realized then that we were amongst those honored for being of some sort of help on that tragic day. Like Saul, some of them were accompanied by family. In that moment I realized that Saul was now just that; my family.

When I looked back to the main room, the crowd had grown significantly. All seats were taken and people were standing off to the sides. The double doors to the room were opened wide and people were also gathered there. The ambient temperature had risen and I soon felt cool air circulating, accompanied by the gentle hum of an air conditioning system. People spoke in hushed voices and I could hear the occasional sob of someone experiencing deep grief. I held onto Saul's hand that much harder.

Soon, the hushed voices began to trail off as a middle aged lady carrying a violin walked up the center aisle. She took a seat behind the podium, well behind the tiny coffin and all of the flowers. She began playing a mournful, slow type of music. The tune was vaguely familiar but I couldn't quite place it. I had only been to one funeral before, but the music had been piped in through speakers. This was much more personal. The older couple sitting by the man and his little girl looked devastated, and the woman began crying quietly.

After the melody ended, an older gentleman stood from the front row and walked to the podium. He arranged a few papers before he began to speak.

"Today is a day of mourning, but also of celebration of the lives of Virginia Hathaway and baby Grace-Anna Hathaway. One of the hardest parts of my job as a man of God is to explain the loss of a child. Of an infant. An innocent baby. How can I sit and tell parents that it was 'God's will'? How can I explain why God would take such a precious life from our world to hold in His arms in Heaven?" The man stopped speaking and looked down at his stack of papers. I could tell he was struggling. He cleared his throat and began again. "I don't always have the words. I don't always have the answers. I've been pastor and friend to the Hathaway family for many years now. I baptized little Virginia when she herself was a baby. I baptized baby Grace-Anna just weeks ago. Never in my wildest dreams did I think that God would call either of them home this soon. Rest assured, though, that they are both in His kingdom now, walking streets of gold and looking down over Jason: husband and father. And over big sister Angela. Virginia was a Godly woman. A devoted wife and a loving mother. She came to speak to me one day, before Grace-Anna was born. She told me that the greatest gift she'd ever been given wasn't that of her own life, but rather that of her children. She was a teacher and role model to so many in our community. When she held that sweet baby or looked at young Angela, her eyes lit up. Her heart soared." He took another deep breath and I could tell he was fighting tears. "If someone needed help, she was always willing. Heaven is a brighter place with her and baby Grace-Anna. That I do believe. Mourning is for us still living. For those of us left behind. We cry for what we have lost. We should celebrate the lives they lived while here on earth, and we should celebrate the fact that they are staring at the face of God at this very moment. Yes, we should celebrate, but God gave us the ability to feel sadness and despair. In our grief, the best we can do is to try to remember what a blessing we were given in their brief lives; however short they were. And that one day, we will see them again. Family has asked to speak, so I'll turn the podium over to Jason. After he speaks, we welcome first other family and then friends to speak if they wish. Jason?" The pastor looked to the man who was comforting the little girl.

The man took his hand from his daughter, and who I assumed was her grandfather took her other hand in his while Jason walked to the podium. His hair was dark and slightly disheveled. His shirt was wrinkled.

"Thank you, everyone, for coming today." He spoke slowly, and I could tell he was fighting to hold himself together. "There's a lot I want to say, and I wrote it down. I knew I'd probably have trouble remembering to tie my own shoes today, let alone remember everything I want to say. I lost my wife that day. I lost the mother of my children. I lost my sweet baby Gracie not even two days later."

He closed his eyes and slumped forward against the podium and took a shuddering breath. I saw someone near him in age and with similar features stand from the front row and walk toward him. Jason held his hand out to indicate that he wanted to continue.

"I want to thank a Good Samaritan for giving me that extra time with my baby girl. I know he's here today, but I don't know his name or what he looks like. But I know he's here today."

Jason looked at the audience, then over to our alcove. I squeezed Saul's hand.

"I need to see you, if you could please stand? Just let me thank you in person. For giving me my Gracie for another day."

Saul stood, letting go of my hand. Jason smiled weakly and gestured for him to come forward. When they were within arm's reach, they shook hands. Jason followed with a desperate hug and began sobbing as he mumbled 'thank you' over and over. Saul held onto the man as he began to slump to the ground, eventually helping him stand back up. Jason was unable to speak, so Saul stood next to him at the podium.

"My name's Saul. I was the one who ran back in and took baby Grace from the fire. Her mother was screaming for someone to help her baby. By the time I got to Grace, I wasn't able to go back for her mom. I wish so badly I could have saved them both. Maybe I could have given them each another day. I wish to God that they both could have lived. So many lives were lost. It's just...senseless." Saul hung his head and I saw him wipe away a tear from his eye. "I wish I had words of comfort," he continued. "Mr. Hathaway. Angela. I'm so sorry for your loss. I'm so sorry."

I could hear the little girl who was sitting across the room from us whimper. Her grandfather stood and lifted her into his arms, carrying her from the service.

The man who shared features with Jason stood again and took the place of both Jason and Saul. As Saul resumed his seat next to me, I leaned against my lover and we took comfort in each other's presence. I could tell he was shaken. The rest of the service lasted an hour; so many people spoke. Virginia and baby Grace were well loved and I could tell would be desperately missed.

CHAPTER 19 ~ SHARING SAUL

The funeral service lasted a lot longer than I had expected; not that I had really known what to expect. I hadn't realized, either, that there would be a graveside service directly following. As we walked across the lush green grass of the cemetery, I was glad I had opted to not wear high heels. The sun was shining and birds were twittering almost as if singing to the lost baby.

The violinist again played a song, this time with a slightly happier tune. I know that words were said and I know that people cried, but I have no recollection of exact sentiments. My attention had been too focused on the tiny coffin. Saul kept an arm around my shoulders the entire time. There were too many people in attendance to rush our exit, so once the crowd was dismissed we stood with Joe and Justine beside our car. Saul's truck had been left where he first parked it a few blocks from the funeral home. We had decided to all go in one vehicle to dinner after the service.

Jason Hathaway, with young Angela in tow, approached us. It was hard to imagine what they were going through. I listened as Mr. Hathaway again thanked Saul for saving his baby and giving them precious extra time with her before she died. I looked down at little Angela. She looked so very scared and sad. I knelt down and took her hands in mine as her father was giving a business card to Saul.

"Hi Angela," I said quietly.

"Hello," she said in a tiny high-pitched voice.

"My name's Hattie."

"I'm Angela, but most people call me Angie. My mommy and baby sister died."

Her eyes were filling with tears and as one began to roll down her cheek I took the handkerchief out of my clutch and dabbed at it.

"Did you know that when I was a little girl my mommy died too?"

The little girl shook her head side to side. "What happened?"

"When my twin brother and I were born something happened that made her very sick. She died when we were only a couple of hours old."

"Do you remember her?" asked the little girl.

"I was too little to remember her. But, my daddy gave me pictures of her so that I will always know what she looked like and this necklace and these earrings were hers. When I wear them it's kind of like she's here with me. And I know that your mommy loved you very much and will be watching over you and your daddy."

Angela looked up at her father and tugged at his suit jacket. "Daddy, Daddy! I need mommy's earrings and necklace!"

Mr. Hathaway leaned down and scooped the girl up into his arms. "I'm sure I have the perfect ones for you at home, Munchkin."

"Now, Daddy! We have to go get them now!" she said with desperation in her little voice.

"What's the rush, Babydoll?"

"If I wear her necklace and earrings I'll feel her with me."

I reached my hand out to touch the girl on the shoulder. "Ahh, sweetie, you'll feel her with you anytime you need her to be there. See how sunny it is?"

The little girl nodded and looked up to the blue sky.

"Then close your eyes," said Saul. "Do you feel the heat on your face?"

The girl clenched her eyes shut. "Yes," whispered Angela.

"That's your mama shining her light down on you. Straight from Heaven," he whispered.

How Saul knew what I was going to tell the little girl, I had no idea. Angela let go of her father and reached out for Saul to take her in his arms, which he did without hesitation. She hugged him tight and began sobbing. I looked over at Joe and Justine, who were both in tears. The line of cars was beginning to move and Mr. Hathaway took Angela from Saul.

"We need to get going, Munchkin. We're having a private family reception afterward, but of course you guys are welcome to join us," said Mr. Hathaway.

Saul extended his hand to the man. "We appreciate the offer, but this is a time for true family."

"Call me in the next few days? Just...keep in touch?" asked the widower.

Little Angie looked at Saul with her big watery eyes. "Will you come play with me sometime?" she asked pitifully.

"You bet, if it's okay with your daddy."

"Hattie will you come too?" she asked, breaking her gaze from Saul only briefly.

"Sure, Angie. Sure I will."

"I'll tell you what; Hattie and I are leaving town tomorrow for a little while. I'll bring you back something really nice, and come over to deliver it myself as soon as we're home," said Saul while looking at Mr. Hathaway for his approval.

"That'd be real nice. We'll have you over for dinner. Just call when you get back?" said Mr. Hathaway.

"You bet. See ya later, gator," said Saul as he pretended to steal the little girl's nose.

As her dad carried her to their car, she waved back at us. "Bye Saul. Bye Hattie! Have a good trip!"

"That poor thing," whispered Justine. I had almost forgotten she and Joe were there. "You did so good with her."

"Let's get moving, huh?" interrupted Joe.

I wrapped my arms around Saul briefly before we ducked into the car and let Joe drive us into Anacortes for dinner.

***

We settled on a small Italian restaurant that was known for good food, good service, and a quiet atmosphere. It was dimly lit and smelled of garlic. Once seated, we ordered drinks and Saul agreed to split an order of lasagna with me. While I was hungry, I knew I wouldn't be able to eat much after the intense emotions the day had brought.

Joe cleared his throat once we had all placed our orders. "So, you two are headed out of town tomorrow?"

Saul sipped at his water before answering. "I thought Hattie could use some time away. Try to deal with all the after effects of the explosion."

"Where are you headed?" asked Justine, who was sipping on her 7-Up that had just arrived.

"Maui," answered Saul as the waiter handed him a beer.

Joe whistled. "Yikes. Serious?"

"He insisted," I mumbled into my water glass.

"That'll be a first," said my brother. "You excited?"

I nodded. "Yeah. It'll be nice to get away. Hey, there's something else I need to talk to you and Justine about. Don't freak out, okay?"

"Uh-oh," said Justine, wide-eyed.

"What is it, Hat?" asked Joe, leaning forward and looking worried. I noticed he glanced at Saul with not the nicest of expressions. "You're not knocked up, are you?"

I briefly choked on my own spit before being able to answer. "No, Joe! God. It's nothing bad."

Saul placed his hand on my thigh beneath the table. "Hattie and I talked and she's decided to move in with me."

"Move in? Doesn't it seem a bit soon?" asked Joe.

"Yeah we know," I said. "But it makes sense. I know we barely just met, but it's like it was fate that we did. We want to be together…and you guys need room for the baby."

"Aww, Hat, that's really sweet," said Justine. "But it's your house too. We can move out just as easily."

"No. I want you to raise the baby there. For as long as you want." I looked over at Saul. "And this is what I want; to live with Saul."

Joe hung his head in thought for a moment. "I'm not sure it's the best decision, sis. But it's yours to make. We'll support your choice, but you're always welcome in your own home. You understand, right?"

"Of course I do."

Joe looked Saul straight in the eyes from across the table. "And you better not hurt her. Understand?"

Saul smiled. "Loud and clear."

"Okay, glad we got that out of the way." Joe's demeanor instantly relaxed. "Did I hear right that you leave tomorrow? For Hawaii?"

I looked at Saul for confirmation. He hadn't given me any details and I hadn't realized he had already booked things.

"At eleven in the morning. We'll leave out of SeaTac," said Saul.

"Do you need a ride to the airport? My schedule's open."

"Actually, I'd appreciate that, Joe. Thanks," said Saul as the waiter arrived with our dinner order.

Looking at the food, my stomach growled. I ended up eating most of the order, leaving Saul very little. He assured me it was okay, that he was fine. We stayed and talked with my brother and his new wife for nearly an hour before deciding to call it a night.

On the drive back to Fidalgo Bay, Saul and I sat in the back seat. We talked quietly, and I leaned against him the entire drive.

"So we'll be in Hawaii tomorrow night?" I whispered to him.

"Uh-huh."

"How'd you get tickets so last minute?"

"I have my secrets," he said with a wink.

"Tomorrow's a week," I said with a smile.

"Uh-huh. It sure is." He wrapped an arm around me and pulled me closer, kissing top of my head. "You look beautiful today, by the way."

"I'm not even sure what to pack. I should probably head home and get ready there. Joe and I could pick you up in the morning."

"Sounds good, except I'll miss you tonight."

"How long will we be gone?"

"Two weeks in paradise, sweet thing. Just pack a bikini and some lingerie and that should do it."

"I heard that," said Joe from the front seat.

Saul chuckled. "Seriously, the resort I booked has laundry in the rooms so you don't need to bring too much. Just remember you can't carry on liquids onto the plane unless each is under three ounces, and you have to pack them into a quart-sized Ziploc baggie. Two carry-ons each and we can check anything bigger."

"Hey Joe, can I borrow your luggage set?" I called up front.

"Sure, sis."

Saul began stroking my hair, which I found soothing.

"You'll love the place we're staying. It's right on Ka'anapali Beach and not far from Black Rock and the Ioa Valley. There's great snorkeling and tons of sea turtles. It's a bit past humpback season, but if we're lucky we might see one or two."

"How many times have you been there?"

"Just a few. It's one of my favorite places. My folks took me there when I was a little boy and I've gone back by myself a few times. The resort has three swimming pools and three or four hot tubs. Oh and a cool kiddie pool with a pirate ship theme."

"You were really good with Angela after the service," I whispered, finding his hand and grabbing onto it.

"She's a cutie. I feel horrible for her and her dad."

We drove the rest of the way in silence. Saul drove himself home and I remained in Joe's car. I packed what I figured I'd need, which wasn't much. Being low maintenance overall, I settled on two bikinis, four pairs of shorts, a skirt, a few t-shirts, one blouse, under things, and a pair of sandals. The suitcase was the smaller kind on wheels, and I would carry it aboard the plane instead of checking anything. I packed a smaller bag with two paperbacks, some Kleenex, my hair brush, lip balm, my iPhone charger, and my next two birth control patches. I added a small lap blanket for the flight. After setting out a sundress in which to travel, a matched set of white lace bra and panties, and sparkly flip-flops, I climbed into bed and tried to force myself to sleep. An unusual mixture of sadness from the day and excitement about the next made sleep difficult.

CHAPTER 20 ~ FLYING HIGH

It was a long drive to the airport, upward of two hours. We had left early to allow for plenty of time for going through security and finding the right gate. Joe had seemed somewhat disgruntled and hadn't said much on the drive. Justine had stayed home to rest before she was due to start her shift at two o'clock that afternoon.

Joe pulled up to the curb labeled 'departures' and Saul and I hustled to grab our bags from the trunk of the car. Joe grumbled something about being glad he'd be back home in time to drive Justine to work. He hadn't found a new vehicle since the explosion had totaled his and was still driving hers. I forced him to give me a quick hug goodbye and was glad to see him shake Saul's hand. It had been several years since my one and only trip on an airplane and I was starting to feel nervous.

"You have your ID, right?" asked Saul for the fourth time.

"My driver's license."

"Since we don't have any bags to check through, we can head straight to the gate."

We both pulled our rolling suitcases with our smaller bags resting on top near the handles. The airport was already bustling with travelers and I made sure to stay near to Saul. Before we had walked very far we came to the security desk where they checked our preprinted boarding passes and ID. After letting us through the checkpoint we made our way to the luggage scanners where Saul insisted on lifting my bags for me. We placed our shoes, cell phones, his wallet, and my purse into a plastic bin before sending it through the scanner. After walking through the metal detector one-by-one, we retrieved all of our items and followed the sign that read 'C-Gates.' We walked down a wide, short hallway until the sign directed us to the right. We immediately came to a bank of sliding glass doors that refused to open.

"What's this thing?" I asked.

"SeaTac's a huge airport, love. This here's a train-thing."

"A train-thing, huh?"

"Uh-huh. A train-thing."

As he looked over at me and smiled the 'train-thing' appeared and the automatic sliding doors opened. Several people filed off in a noisy rush and just as quickly we stepped into the tram. Overhead a computerized voice told us to sit down or hold onto something securely. There were gray plastic seats facing each other on either side of the tram and metal poles ran down the center of the cars, spaced about every four feet. Several other people had boarded with us and I decided to stand and hold onto a pole to allow younger children and the elderly to sit. Saul stood close behind me, wrapping his arms around me and holding on to the pole just below where my hands were placed. Our luggage was tucked neatly by our feet. The train sped away with a slight jolt. I must have tensed because Saul kissed me on the cheek and whispered to me that he was excited to get into my pants later.

***

We sat at a Starbucks and drank coffee until it was almost time to board our flight. Once to the gate, we sat off to one corner waiting for our turn to board the plane. I was surprised when Saul stood when they called for first class passengers.

"Saul?" I asked.

"That's us, babe."

"First class?"

"Uh-huh."

"Oh my God. The tickets must have cost a fortune!"

"Uh-huh. But don't worry about it. My Grandpa would have insisted on only the best for such a pretty girl as yourself," he said with a wink.

He offered me his hand, which I took as I stood. We gathered our bags and walked to the roped-off area that would lead us to the plane. We presented our boarding passes to the man scanning them and then proceeded down the jet way and eventually onto the plane. We settled into our seats, which were located in the very first row. They were dark blue with burgundy trim and unexpectedly comfortable. Saul stowed our luggage in the overhead bin before joining me in the seats. Passenger after passenger filed onto the plane, most looking excited.

***

After a quick safety demonstration by the flight crew we were in-air and underway. The flight lasted nearly six hours, landing later than scheduled. The captain had explained that the delay was due to strong headwinds. I hadn't been bothered by the delay because it had been time spent just being near Saul. The flight had been smooth and we spent most of the time talking about our childhoods, our hopes, our dreams, even life regrets. For one day, I found my thoughts to be less focused on recent tragic events.

As soon as our plane came to a stop at the Kahului airport, Saul stood and retrieved our bags. We were the first two passengers to disembark. Our first steps off the plane brought us to a small uncovered section of jet way. The sun was shining and the air felt, and smelled, different. It was pleasantly warm; almost hot. Saul told me that the scent was wild plumeria. Once we entered the airport itself, we crossed the gate to an outdoor hallway that was built of brick. Saul pointed at lush green trees nearby that bore beautiful white flowers. We walked hand-in-hand down the corridor, each pulling our luggage behind us. Several people walked toward us, obviously on their way to an outbound flight. They were all tan and looked sad to be leaving. Before long the corridor ended at an inside circular area that led in four different directions. We followed the sign to "baggage claim/rental cars." After a quick escalator ride down one level, we entered a large room that housed several luggage carousels. A young woman stood off to the left holding a sign that said "Meyers."

"That's us, babe," said Saul, gesturing toward the woman with his head.

The woman smiled when she saw him. "Saul, so good to see you!"

"Tina, thanks so much for picking us up. This is Hattie," he said as he wrapped an arm around me.

Tina extended her hand to me, and I took it with a smile.

"Hattie, Tina's my buddy's sister. They're from the islands."

"Nice to meet you, Tina," I said.

"So glad Saul brought you here," she directed toward me. "Saul, Brock's in town. He says to come over for a luau before you head back to Seattle."

Saul beamed at the news. "We will, for sure. Have him call me in a couple days? We'll arrange it."

"Good, you can meet my fiancé when you come!" said Tina.

I found the news of a fiancé relieving and felt myself relax. Tina was a natural beauty. I wasn't sure if she was native or not, but her dark skin looked sun-kissed and her black hair was long and shiny. Her features were petite and I could tell that her personality shined as well.

"You're getting married? That's great! He better treat you well?" said Saul.

Tina smiled, making her striking features stand out even more. "He does. His name's Suko, by the way. You'll like him."

"I better," grumbled Saul with a wink.

"Ok, let's get you guys to your little resort paradise. Just drop me off at home?"

"It's the least we can do. I really appreciate the car loan."

"Be good to my baby, ok?" said Tina said, indicating the car.

"You know it, girl."

We followed Tina out into the bright sunshine. Three crosswalks later, we arrived at her car. I was a bit surprised to see it was old, and only had two seats.

"Uh, Tina?" I asked.

"Huh?"

"It's cute but how will all three of us fit?"

She chuckled, and from Saul's expression I could tell he was wondering the same thing.

"Teen, where's your Ford Focus?"

"Oh that piece of crap? I wrecked it. No worries...I was kidding about taking me home. Suko's picking me up in a few minutes."

Saul hugged her. "You brat."

"Ok, so it's a 1975 MGB. Glad you didn't bring much luggage cause the trunk's small. The top's manual so put it up at night in case it rains. It's not hard to figure out. The wipers can be a bit tricky, but if they won't work just turn the engine off then restart it and they usually work again." She held a key out to Saul. "Keep it unlocked at night so no one slashes the top, okay? You never know when someone might try to break in and look for hidden treasures."

"Thanks, Teen. We'll take good care of her."

Tina opened the small trunk and I saw she hadn't been kidding. The tiny spare tire took up most of the space. Saul was able to fit one rolling suitcase and both smaller bags inside the back end, and the other rolling case fit nicely in the small space behind the only two seats.

As soon as our luggage was stowed, a motorcycle pulled up. A handsome man waved to Tina.

"That's Suko. I'll introduce you when you guys come over. He's in a hurry to get to work."

Tina skittered off and straddled the bike. She took a helmet from her man and put it on as he was speeding away.

"Ah, just the two of us now," said Saul as he leaned down and kissed me.

"She seems nice," I said.

"Her whole family is. You'll like them."

"How do you know them?"

"I met her brother, Brock, when I worked up in Alaska for a summer. Fishing."

"Ah. Cool. What kind of fishing?"

"Deep sea crab," he said as he held my car door open for me.

I slid into the little bucket seat and fastened the seatbelt around myself. I took my sunglasses from on top of my head and put them on my face as Saul took his place behind the wheel. I watched as he started the engine and grinned at me.

"I hope you don't mind me borrowing the MG from Tina. I thought it'd be a lot more fun than a stuffy rental car."

"No, it's fine. Looks like fun," I answered.

"You ready, babe?"

I was growing warm sitting in the direct sun and nodded in reply.

"It's about a forty-five minute drive to the Villas. Do you want to go straight there or stop at a beach along the way?"

"Oh, can we stop at the beach?" I asked excitedly.

"We can. But not for long because I'm dying to get inside of you."

I felt my insides tingle in response to his desire. "To the resort, then."

***

The drive to the Westin Villas only took about half an hour since Saul went a bit faster than the speed limit. I had never ridden in a convertible before and the entire drive was a thrill. The entry to the resort was lined with plumeria and palm trees and lower growing tropical shrubs. The asphalt roadways were dark and bordered by lighter colored sidewalks. As Saul turned to the right with the curve of the road I took notice of an ornate long-canoe on display. Within a few more seconds he turned to his left and into a circular drive, where he parked the car.

"Okay, Hattie Cakes, this is our stop."

I grinned like a school girl, excited about our adventure. Before I could open my door one of the resort staff opened it for me.

"Aloha!" said a dark-skinned man wearing a string of shells around his neck, white shorts, and a tropical short-sleeved shirt in hues of white and beige. "Welcome to Paradise!"

Saul quickly stood. "Mahalo!"

I had no idea what 'mahalo' meant, but since he said it with a smile I assumed it was good.

"Are you checking in today, sir?" asked the man.

"We are." Saul walked around to my side of the car and handed the man the car keys, and I noted he slipped the man a folded green bill along with the keys.

"Mahalo," said the staff to him. "My name's Henry. If you need anything, feel free to ask for me or any other member of our staff. I'll get your car parked while you check in."

"Thanks, friend, and aloha," said Saul as he shook Henry's hand.

We fetched our meager bags from the trunk and the space behind the seats, and I followed Saul through a large open area that led to a grand lobby. There were clean damp washcloths set out on a table to our right. Saul told me they were for freshening up hands and face after a long, hot journey. There was also a large clear glass cooler filled with ice water and slices of pineapple. I had never seen anywhere so lavish in my life. Saul stopped at the table and filled two small plastic cups with water.

"You have to try this," he whispered. "It's tradition."

I gladly took the icy beverage and sipped at it. It smelled of pineapple, with just a faint taste of fruit. I drank the rest thirstily, not caring if it was unladylike. Once we had both finished two glasses, we proceeded inside and to the large reception desk. There were five "stations" for checking in, and we were the only guests at the moment. Another tan woman with dark hair, wearing similar clothes as Henry out front, smiled when she saw us. Her hair was pulled back and on the right side of her bun was a large tropical flower. I knew right then that I had to have one before the trip was over.

"Mr. Meyers, good to see you back!" said the woman, whose name badge read "Rose."

"You too, Rose."

"We have your suite all ready for you. Two weeks this time, in an ocean view studio? Does that sound right?"

"That sounds perfect. Thanks, Rosie."

"Okay, it's room 7-632. Would you like a map?"

"Just one, please."

"And how many room keys?"

"Two should do it."

"And towel cards?"

"Let's do four."

"Very good. We still have your credit card on file, if you can verify the last four digits?"

Saul pulled his wallet out and found a red-colored plastic card. "8012."

"Perfect. You're all set, then. If you need anything at all please let us know."

Rose handed Saul a map of the resort grounds with our room circled in pen, and a small envelope that contained plastic cards.

"Mahalo, Rosie."

"Have a wonderful stay, Mr. and Mrs. Meyers."

I blushed at her assumption on who I was.

We rolled our suitcases across the lobby, where Saul took me aside to a railing that overlooked a large koi pond one story down. Palm trees dotted the courtyard and in the distance I caught a glimpse of the ocean. I smiled.

Soon we took an elevator to the sixth floor, where we found building seven and eventually our room. Once inside, I cleared my throat.

"Okay, Saul. Spill the beans. They know you here."

He chuckled. "It's not a big deal. Grandpa left a timeshare to me and Lina. Usually we each use two of the four weeks in one of these studios. It really has everything we need, but we could do two weeks total in a one-bedroom. I figured we could use both weeks in the smaller room."

"And you get to do this every year?" I asked, a bit overwhelmed.

"I guess so. The timeshare's paid for through I think 2030."

"Holy cow."

He had set his bags off to one side of the door, and gently took mine from me. "Have a quick look around before I get you naked?" he said as he began kissing my neck. "You already taste like flowers and sunshine," he groaned. "And honey."

I kissed him back and then teased him by pushing him away a bit. "Let me use the bathroom first?"

He sighed dramatically. "Okay, okay. If you insist. It's on your left."

I walked around him, gently sliding my hand across the crotch of his jeans as I did so.

"Oh my GOD!" I shrieked. "The bathtub!"

I heard him chuckle.

"It's huge!" I added.

Unable to resist, I set the plug in the bottom of the tub and turned the hot water on. The bathtub and sink were in a large bathroom with a sliding door made of tempered glass framed in cherry wood. The shower and toilet were in a smaller room across from the tub, with its own sliding door. Above the bathtub was a bi-fold partition meant for privacy between the bedroom area and the bathroom. It was unlike anything I had ever seen before. Plush white towels in various sizes were on a shelf beneath the sink and the counter had a little supply of green tea and aloe soaps and hair care products. While the bathtub was filling, I did my business in the room housing the toilet and stripped out of my sundress while in there. I left my bra and panties on, knowing they'd drive Saul wild.

"Saul?" I called from behind the privacy glass of the small door.

"Yeah babe?"

"Can you bring me a glass of water?"

"Uh. Sure. Ice?"

"Actually, just a glass of ice would be perfect."

"Just ice? No water?"

"Just ice. Thanks."

I snuck out of the small shower room until I was standing beside the tub, nearly nude. I checked the temperature of the water with my fingertips, and was glad it wasn't too hot, or cold. I shut the faucet off prematurely, the bathtub only about a third full. I could hear the clinking of ice cubes as Saul filled a glass and waited for him to appear. As he rounded the corner and saw me, his eyes took on a glazed-over appearance.

"God, you're gorgeous," he whispered.

He had taken off his shirt and shorts and stood in just boxer shorts. The muscles of his chest had never looked as tempting as they did then, and his excitement was clearly obvious by how tight his undershorts had become.

I slowly walked to him, keeping my gaze on his chest, and did my best to play 'innocent.' I slowly slid the index finger of my right hand down his chest, causing him to shiver. The smell of the green tea and jasmine body wash I had added to the bath water swirled around us. I could feel Saul's gaze upon me, but kept my eyes on the flesh of his chest.

"I thought maybe we could take a bath," I whispered. "But the water might be too hot."

I carefully glanced at the glass of ice he still held, and slowly took one of the cubes out with my left hand, never taking my right from his flesh. After a forced sigh, I slowly turned my head up to meet his gaze. He wore a look that just barely hinted at fear mixed with longing and humor. I carefully placed one end of the ice cube gently against his left pectoral, and waited for him to react. Instead of flinching, he closed his eyes and his breathing deepened. I trailed the ice down toward his navel and as a small drip of melted water ran down his happy trail he gasped.

"Holy shit," he groaned.

"You like?" I whispered as I repeated the motion of the ice, this time starting on his other pectoral.

"I love. Oh Lord, Hattie."

He leaned down and kissed me with passion. I felt him reach toward the counter behind me and heard him set the glass of ice down. I wasn't aware that he had taken the single ice cube from me until I heard it added back to the glass. His mouth worked at my neck, gently but eagerly, and soon I felt my bra loosen. It fell to the floor and Saul backed away to gaze at my bared breasts. His hands soon stripped me of the matching panties and he carried me around the corner to the king-sized bed that was dressed in white linens and pillows.

"It's been a week," he grumbled against my belly as he lay me down on the bed.

I scooted back on the bed as he removed his boxers.

"A week exactly," I said quietly.

"Is it okay if we try something different this time?" he asked.

I licked my lips and nodded.

He crawled toward me and kissed me again. As he broke the kiss, he turned me over onto my belly and whispered for me to scoot onto my hands and knees. I did, feeling just a bit embarrassed to give him such a view of my backside. My embarrassment faded as soon as I heard him moan in pleasure at the sight. He situated himself behind me and reached around to pull my hair back from my face. One of his hands smoothed my hair down my back as the other reached around to cup one of my breasts. The anticipation of him entering me was becoming unbearable and I whimpered.

"Does this feel okay so far?" he asked quietly.

"Uh huh."

His hand moved from my breast to my belly, and slowly to my clit. He used a fingertip to gently caress me there, causing me to moan.

"Still feel okay?" he asked, his voice strained.

"Uh huh," I squeaked.

He leaned forward and kissed me on the small of my back, and then moved into position to enter me. I could feel his hard cock between my legs. His erection was smooth and hot. It felt so much better than with a condom and I groaned from the pleasure. He teased me for a moment, rubbing the head of his penis against my already moist lips. His finger resumed caressing my clit and finally he entered me, more deeply than he had before. The sensation was breathtaking and I came far sooner than I had meant to. He continued to thrust rhythmically, and fell apart inside of me only moments after I had. Completely spent, we fell asleep holding each other.

CHAPTER 21 ~ BUBBA GUMPS

Our first full day in Hawaii was spent being lazy: lounging by the pools and taking an occasional dip in the hot tub. The sun was bright with only the occasional white cloud drifting by. Saul bought a floating air mattresses from one of the pool-side shacks, as well as a bottle of coconut oil. After we had enjoyed a morning Mai Tai while lying in our chaise lounge chairs pool-side, Saul rubbed me down with the tropical oil. He said it was tradition and would help us tan, but I knew he was enjoying if for very different reasons. I had chosen a bright yellow bikini to wear for the day, which covered just enough of me to allow Saul to use his imagination as to what was underneath. My skin was painfully pale white, so I hoped the oil wouldn't cause me to burn too badly. If nothing else, I enjoyed the coconut smell and the feel of Saul's strong hands rubbing it into my skin.

By noon we were both starving for both lunch and each other. We returned to our villa and quickly ordered room service: two Cokes and two burgers with fries. We were told it would arrive in about half an hour. During that time my yellow bikini managed to find its way to the floor, along with Saul's bright blue board shorts. The excitement of not knowing if we'd finish by the time the food arrived was oddly arousing.

After lunch and a lazy nap, we headed back to the pools, where I floated on the air mattress while Saul swam nearby. A breeze had picked up, which I welcomed as the heat seemed more intense this side of the sun, so to speak. The motion of the air mattress floating had me near asleep when Saul suddenly pounced on the side of the floatation device. I shrieked when I rolled off and into the water with him. Saul grabbed me around the waist and pulled me closer. His arms were strong and reassuring and his skin smelled of the sun. I allowed myself to relax in his arms, more content than I had been in a long time. He put his forehead against mine as we enjoyed the moment of closeness.

"Marry me, Hattie," he whispered. His voice was sincere and strong, and filled with desperation. I shivered in his arms. Not from being cold, but rather from the effect he had on me. He kept his forehead against mine and closed his eyes, slowly inhaling and waiting. "Please," he whispered.

"Saul…"

"Shhh. Don't answer. I don't want to spoil the day with a 'no'."

When I began to speak again, he hushed me with a deep, passionate kiss.

"Saul, stop," I mumbled against him.

He looked at me, hurt. I placed my hands on either side of his face and looked at him lovingly.

"Yes, Saul."

He looked confused.

"Yes, I'll marry you!"

He looked stunned for a few moments while what I had said sunk in. "You will?" he asked, still looking like a sad puppy dog.

"Yes," I repeated. "I'll marry you."

Finally, a grin spread across his face and he lifted me halfway out of the water in a huge hug.

"Thank you," he said, sounding on the verge of tears. "I swear as long as I live I'll love and adore you."

We kissed again, until the sounds of children playing "Marco Polo" reminded us where we were.

"Let's go to dinner to celebrate?" he asked hopefully.

I nodded. "Okay."

"Let's get ready. We need to stop somewhere on the way."

I smiled. He was like a child on Christmas morning, and it warmed my heart. We retrieved the air mattress that had floated off to the shallow end of the pool and used the stairs to get out of the water. We dried off quickly, turned our wet pool towels in for fresh towel cards, and walked hand-in-hand back to our room.

Saul had said dinner would be casual, so I dressed in a pair of cutoff jean shorts and a tight-fitting v-neck t-shirt in plain white. The ride in the convertible was again a thrill. We headed toward a little town called Lahaina, where Saul swore the best restaurant was a noisy hole-in-the-wall called 'Bubba Gumps,' dedicated to the movie Forrest Gump.

He pulled into a small parking lot across from the restaurant, where a valet took the keys and car from him. Instead of crossing the street, he took hold of my hand and pulled me eagerly to the right, where we entered a small street-front store. When I realized it was a fine jewelry store, my breath caught in my chest.

"Saul, you don't have to..." I began.

"No way, Hattie. You're not taking away my right to buy you something nice."

We continued into the store. It was small, and the glass cases that lined three walls and the sparkling things that surrounded us made me feel underdressed.

"Good evening," said a tall man with gray hair. "How can I help you?"

"We'd like to look at engagement rings, please," said Saul.

The tall man smiled and clapped his hands together once. "Excellent! Congratulations! If you step over here to your left, I'll show you some of what we have in stock. You can also order from our supply of loose stones and have them set in the band of your choice. It only takes about two days, if you're just visiting the island?"

I clung to Saul's arm as we approached the case the man had indicated. I was oddly nervous.

"Do you know what shape and size of stone you might like?" asked the older gentleman.

I bit my lower lip and shook my head side-to-side slowly. "Honestly I have no idea. Nothing too big though."

Saul leaned over and whispered to me. "I want you to pick what you like, babe. Don't worry about the cost."

I looked up at him and forced a smile. I wasn't used to being spoiled.

"May I look at your hands?" asked the clerk.

I held my hands up in front of him.

"You have nice slender fingers, and small hands. I would recommend not going too large on the stone size, or it may look awkward. I think any shape would look beautiful."

I smiled and moved my hands back to my sides. Saul found my right hand with his left and held it lovingly. My eyes were focused on the dozens of rings below the glass.

"Can I see that one there?" I asked, pointing at a yellow band that appeared to have texture near the center stone, which sparkled wildly.

"Ah, good taste," said the man behind the counter as he opened the glass door on his side and removed the ring from its display. He handed me the ring. It felt cool in my palm, and made me smile. It was simple, yet beautiful. The stone was marquis shaped and not too small, yet not too large.

"May I try it on?" I asked.

The salesman grinned. "Of course you may."

I slid the ring onto my left ring finger. Oddly, it was a perfect fit. I held my hand out in front of me and smiled. I knew instantly that it was the ring I wanted. I didn't need to see any others.

"It looks beautiful on you," said Saul quietly.

"Indeed it does," agreed the salesman. "Can I show you a few more?"

"No," I uttered quickly. "This is it. This is the one."

"Hattie, there's at least fifty here to choose from," chuckled Saul.

I looked at him very seriously. "No. This is the right one."

"You sure?" he asked with a worried look.

"Positive. It's the first one that caught my eye and it just feels...right."

"Let me just make sure it doesn't need adjusting?" asked the clerk.

I held my hand out and he wiggled at the ring.

"I don't think it could be a better fit," he said with a kind smile."

"Okay then," said Saul followed by a deep breath. "We'll take it."

"Excellent. I think you'll be very happy with it. It comes with a lifetime warranty, provided you bring it in every twelve months for a check. It's a 0.72 carat diamond, yellow gold with a brushed accent, and of course the wedding band."

"We live on the mainland. Is there anywhere closer to home we can have it checked?" asked Saul.

"Absolutely. Where about do you live?"

"Near Seattle."

"We have two shops we contract with. One in Seattle itself and one in Bellevue. I'll get you their information."

"Thanks," said Saul with a satisfied smile.

I looked at Saul suddenly.

"What's wrong?" he asked.

"I don't have money to buy you one," I pouted.

"Yes you do," he said.

I just stayed quiet as the salesman walked to another glass cabinet, where he took out several different men's bands.

"I'd recommend one of the comfort fit bands. They're rounded on the edges and really are more comfortable. All of these ones here fit the bill, and I have several others if you'd like me to bring them out?"

Saul looked over the choices in front of him. He tried several on and chose one that complemented my set almost perfectly. We left the shop wearing our new gifts to each other, even though he paid for both.

"You're beaming," he said as we walked the short distance to the restaurant.

"Thank you," I said sweetly as I glanced at my ring again.

"You're sure it's the one you want?"

"Positive."

"You're sure I'm the one you want?" he pressed.

"Absolutely positive."

The sun was well toward setting and the evening was cooling off a bit. Saul put our names in at the podium outside of Bubba Gump's and we waited to be called, standing on the sidewalk looking at the huge tree that the building had been built around; a plaque told the story of the massive tree. Eventually we were seated at a small table overlooking the ocean. The surf crashed on the rocks below and the evening breeze blew in gently through the open windows. We didn't say much to each other over dinner, but enjoyed good food and gazing at one another.

***

The short drive back to the resort was made in the dark. We stopped at a public beach along the way to enjoy the effects of a full moon highlighting the waves offshore. We sat for a while in the dry sand, talking about our hopes and dreams. We still had so much to learn about each other, and now a lifetime in which to study each other. Saul told me that his grandfather had been a very wealthy man who had lived a very simple life. He had left his fortune to be split between Saul and Carolina. He wasn't sure exactly how much there was because most of it was invested, but he assured me it was enough for us to live comfortably for a long time. Not a lavish lifestyle, but a comfortable one. He had worked odd jobs, like his fishing gig in Alaska, for years, but his dream was to open a summer camp for special needs kids. As a teenager, his best friend had been from a family who had adopted a little girl with an undiagnosed seizure disorder. She had been badly abused in her first two years of life, and his family had changed her life when they welcomed her into their hearts and home. She had been a glowing star and had loved Saul fiercely. She died when she was eight, and it had devastated him. I talked about what it was like to grow up without a mother, being a twin, and about my hope to own a bakery one day.

The night was turning chilly, so I leaned against Saul for warmth.

"Saul?" I asked as a wave crashed against the shore not far away.

"Yeah babe?"

"I want to get married here."

"This beach?" he asked, sounding perplexed.

"No, just here. Maui. Before we go home."

"Ah, babe, you want your family and friends with you don't you?"

"No, I just need you. We could get married here, now, and have a second wedding back home later. Maybe at the end of summer?"

He looked at me very seriously. "Are you sure?"

I nodded. "I want to leave this place as your wife. I'm a hundred percent sure. Two hundred."

He kissed the top of my head. "You're freezing," he whispered. "We'll head back and talk about it in bed."

"Just don't say no, okay?"

He chuckled as he stood and helped me up.

CHAPTER 22 ~ LUAU

Our two weeks in Maui were nearly at an end. Saul had agreed to be married before we boarded the plane back to Washington. He had made arrangements, all with my approval. Brock and Tina's father was a minister at a small church on the other side of the island and had been delighted to offer to marry us. Tina and her brother, Brock, had joined us at the resort for an afternoon. While Brock and Saul caught up with each other pool-side, Tina took me into Lahaina shopping for a dress. She had squealed over my gorgeous ring and seemed genuinely pleased to see Saul and me getting married. We enjoyed a light lunch at a fish taco truck near the beach, and ended up at an outdoor mall that she explained was a tourist trap. We found my dress at the first shop we tried: a lightweight white beach dress that was well fitted on top and fell loosely to my ankles. It wasn't a bridal gown, but was exactly what I pictured for our big day in paradise. Tina offered to make me a bouquet out of tropical flowers that grew in their yard and I agreed, so long as she promised to keep it simple. Tiny was funny and smart. She began to really grow on me. We talked about her own wedding plans and she begged us to come back for their big day.

At the end of our outing, she drove me to her father's house so I could see where we'd be saying our vows. The property was amazing. A lush green lawn surrounded a humble island home. The landscaping was beautiful with many different kinds of flowers in bloom and birds singing nearby. A gentle slope led down to a beach of white sand. I fell in love with the location and found myself excited to share it with Saul the next day. I was introduced to Mr. Alfonzo, Tina and Brock's father. He was a large man with an even larger smile. He didn't shake my hand, but rather hugged me tight and congratulated me on the upcoming nuptials. Tina disappeared somewhere while her father walked me down to the beach. He worked a fatherly talk in about the importance of marriage, and I could tell that he truly cared about my future with Saul. I was humbled.

Mrs. Alfonzo arrived home just after her husband and I had walked back up the gentle slope of the lawn to the house. She had a large smile like her husband and also hugged me. I was invited inside, where ice tea was served along with fresh fruit. Before long Saul and Brock arrived and we enjoyed a traditional meal of white rice, pickled seaweed, and fried spam for dinner. None of us drank any alcohol, wanting to make sure we were clear-headed for the events of the next day. Saul drove us home after dinner, where we slept deeply until morning.

***

Our next to last day in paradise was as sunny as the rest had been, but was somehow brighter. We packed what we needed into a tote bag that we had bought at the resort gift shop. Our clothing was meant to be worn slightly wrinkled, except for Saul's slacks, and Mrs. Alfonzo assured him that if they needed pressing she'd be thrilled to do so.

The wedding was scheduled for five o'clock to take advantage of the evening light and to avoid the peak heat of the day. The Alfonzo family had already invited several of their local friends who knew Saul for the luau that was being held in our honor. The wedding ceremony had become a bonus. The expanse of lawn that had been wide-open the day before had been transformed into something from a fairy tale. Torches on bamboo poles lined the periphery of the yard, already lit. Off to one side was a large fire pit that had been set up, complete with a staked pig that was slowly cooking. Several long tables had been set up with white table cloths and bouquets of flowers. Shrubs that surrounded the yard twinkled with strings of little white lights.

As soon as we arrived, Tina grabbed me and rushed me into the house to help me get dressed. She was wearing a tropical wrap-dress that went over one shoulder. Her black hair was down over her shoulders with one side swept back and pinned with a real pink hibiscus flower. She looked perfect. She helped me style my hair, also down like hers, but pinned back on both sides. She surprised me with a crown of fresh plumeria flowers. When I saw myself in the mirror, I almost cried. She did my make up for me, which consisted of just powder, eye liner, mascara, and light pink lipstick. Anything more would be useless with the heat and humidity. I carefully undressed and stepped into my dress, allowing Tina to help zip up the back. I could hear familiar voices coming from somewhere inside the small home.

"Tina, who's here?" I asked, curious.

"Hmm. Probably just friends of Brock." She smoothed my hair for me and smiled. "You look beautiful."

"Thanks, Tina. I'll never forget all you've done for us."

"Aw, c'mon…no crying," she said quietly as she gave me a gentle hug.

There was a light knock on the door, and Mrs. Alfonzo snuck in.

"You look beautiful!" she squealed as she looked me over. "A tropical princess!"

"Thank you," I said with a large smile on my face.

"I have something for you. Just a very small gift from our family."

"You're already doing so much," I insisted.

She shushed me gently and held up a beautiful string of large dark brown polished Hawaiian seeds that had been hand painted with white flowers. Each seed was about the size of a grape and separated with a small seashell.

"Oh, Mrs. Alfonzo," I said. "They're beautiful."

"Please, call me Annie. And they pale next to you. You'll find these necklaces for sale all over the island, but they're just cheap knock-offs. These are much better. The real thing."

"Thank you," I said as the woman put them over my head, being careful of my flower crown.

"Everyone's waiting. Are you ready?"

I nodded. "I think so."

"Since your father is not here to walk you down the aisle, we have a substitute waiting. He's in the living room."

"Brock?" I asked.

Mrs. Alfonzo shook her head side to side. "No, Brock's busy standing up for Saul. C'mon, let's get you to the aisle. Tina, don't forget you walk first. Your bouquets are waiting in the front room."

I followed Tina and her mom out of the back bedroom and around the corner to their living room. Standing there, waiting for me, was my brother Joe. He had a large grin on his face and held his arms open for me.

"Joe!" I squealed. "Oh my God, how are you here?"

"Saul sent for us, sis. How could I say no? Congratulations."

He embraced me with the love of a brother.

"We?" I asked.

"Me and Justine. Dad wanted to come. He really did, but Helen pulled her crap."

"Of course she did, but her name isn't allowed on my big day."

I felt him chuckle. "May I walk you down the aisle?"

"It'll make today perfect if you do," I said with a big grin.

The beat of island drums began, which was our signal to walk to the beach. I took hold of the crook of Joe's arm and waited for Tina to walk ahead of us. Annie had already disappeared and I imagined she would meet us at the shore. Joe and I stood on the lawn just outside the house and watched Tina walk away. Once she was out of sight, the beat of the drums quickened. Our signal to proceed. Walking beside Joe toward the man who would become my husband felt like the most natural thing in the world. The grass was cool beneath my bare feet and the simple bouquet in my hands smelled like a touch of heaven. As the beach came into view, Saul looked stunning in his beige slacks and loose white cotton shirt. He was also barefoot and wore a lei of plumeria to match my crown. He beamed when he saw me. A small crowd of witnesses was standing on either side of us once we reached the sand, and Saul and Mr. Alfonzo were closer to the water. Brock and Tina stood nearby, and to my delight I noticed Lina standing next to Tina. I caught a glance of Justine and smiled at her.

Joe passed me off to Saul and the rest of the ceremony was like a dream. Our vows were kept simple, rings were exchanged, and we were pronounced husband and wife. The sun grew lower in the sky, preparing to kiss the horizon as my new husband kissed me to seal our vows. As soon as our lips met, our witnesses clapped and cheered. We enjoyed the luau and danced when we weren't busy chatting with guests. Brock and one of his cousins demonstrated fire dancing. We eventually said our good-bye's to everyone. Saul and I would be leaving for home the next day, but Joe, Justine, and Lina would be staying on for a few days to enjoy a brief vacation.

~*~

EPILOGUE

Saul and I spent the next year in his little seaside cabin, still getting to know each other. He spent a few days a week volunteering at a nearby facility that cared for special needs children. I knew one day he'd realize his dream of opening his own center. His passion for those amazing kids became mine as well, and my dreams of owning a bakery began to fade. The more time went by, the fewer nightmares I had. We had begun visiting little Angela and her father once a week. They became part of our family and together we all began to heal. Life felt good with Saul at my side.

Joe and Justine delivered a beautiful baby boy that fall, who they ended up naming James William. He was the light of their lives. My father said he was the spitting image of our mother. Daddy ended up leaving Helen when he caught her screwing a guy in his thirties. We all felt bad for him, but we were all glad to see her go. She had never truly loved our father, which he finally saw for himself. Baby James helped him in his grief. He moved home to the Pacific Northwest and lived with Joe, Justine, and baby James.

Carolina had moved home to Anacortes and went to work at a local preschool while taking night classes. Her goal was to become a kindergarten teacher. She still bore scars from the murder in Virginia. She and I had a bond, each bearing scars from a tragedy. She had quickly become one of my dearest friends.

Everett had difficulty accepting my marriage to Saul. He didn't try to cause problems for us, but grieved over losing me. Or rather over losing the dream of me and him and a happily ever after. To cope, he joined the Marines. Miranda was devastated, of course, yet proud of her only son. We all feared for him, knowing it was a time of war.

***

It was almost our one year anniversary and we were back in Maui. Tina and Suko were about to be married on the same beach where we had said our own vows. Tina's dad was officiating and excitement was in the air. My heart soared as I remembered our own special day. Saul and I stood in the crowd of excited witnesses waiting for the wedding to begin. He had an arm around my waist and held me close. In my arms I held our beautiful three-month-old daughter, Lulu Grace-Anna. She wriggled in my arms as if dancing to the primitive music, her eyes wide. Seeing her so happy made my heart soar. We hadn't known that she had been with us on our first visit to the island. Our one-time of being careless had led to one of the very best things in our new life together. Slowly, flowers were blooming from the ashes of that tragic day in Fidalgo Bay.

About the Author

Blythe Santiago is the New Adult Romance pen name of horror author M. Lauryl Lewis.

Born, raised, and dedicated to living in the Great Pacific Northwest, she enjoys spending time with her husband and their three little boys. Favorite hobbies include camping, reading, and of course writing. She is a full-time author, recently retired from her career as an RN.

Connect with her at:

@MLaurylLewis
http://mlauryllewis.blogspot.com
https://www.facebook.com/MLaurylLewis

Made in the USA
Charleston, SC
26 February 2014